Shifting to Black

Barb Shadow

This book is dedicated to my mom, smiling down and keeping an eye on things, and my dad, who would have been so proud.

1

Dom parked his van and grabbed the laptop from the backseat. Thumbing through its case, he made sure he had all the paperwork and notes he would need when he met with his team. *His* team. He liked that. It had taken a long time to get to where he was, with people who worked well together. He watched the street, hand on the door handle, waiting for a break in traffic. Even on a Sunday afternoon the town was bustling. When the traffic paused at the red light, he stepped out and circled to the back of his van. He ran his hand through his hair, letting it fall over his ears, and slung the laptop over his shoulder.

Without glancing back, he hit the lock button on his keyring. There was nothing in the van worth stealing but the habit remained. Secure. It was a good feeling. He looked up at the red brick apartment building in front of him. Tall and typical of the city; ivy growing up the sides with bricks radiating the summer heat. Brown-red, like warm charcoal briquettes. He took the front steps two by two, passing planters with flowers that were well past their prime. It hadn't rained in a week and their stems were cracked and brown. The blooms had long since fallen onto the cement landing, frail and clingy as if gasping for their last breath. He hit the buzzer for apartment twelve.

"Yo!" came the reply, accompanied by a long buzz. He pushed the door open and continued up the green painted stairwell. Emerging into the hallway, he turned right and then left down a longer hall. The usual apartment ambience. Beige, nondescript carpeting to hide the tracked in dirt. Easy to vacuum, if anyone ever went through with that intent. He doubted they did. There were some lights at either end of the corridor, wrapped in metal cages to keep the yellowing bulbs safe. He stopped at number twelve and knocked.

"Yeah!!"

Dom swung the metal door open, walked in and deposited his laptop on the couch. "Hey! How's it going?"

Brian raised his can of Coke in acknowledgement and nodded at the television. He was sitting on a black leather couch, leaning with his arms on his knees. The air conditioner whirred in the background, drapes drawn across the sliding glass door to the balcony. The show finished and Brian sat back. Credits were rolling over a black and gray backdrop of tombstones.

"You see the new ghost series yet? Not bad, but we could give 'em some pointers."

"Yeah?"

"Hell, yeah. These guys…" he pointed at the TV with his soda can, "amateurs."

Dom laughed. He liked Brian, especially with his twenty-something enthusiasm. At thirty-eight, Dom was calmer, more mature.

"No joke," Brian said. "So, what's this new case you mentioned? Something good?" He turned toward Dom, placing his drink on the floor at his feet. He was barefoot and in an old pair of denim shorts. Dom wondered how he could stand the leather on the backs of his thighs. Sticking to it would make him crazy.

"Oh, you're going to love this one. Got a call from a realtor trying to sell a murder house."

Brian's eyes lit up. "Really?" Dom could see the wheels turning in his brain. Spinning. Brian was their tech guy and Dom knew he was already planning, plotting out the equipment they should bring.

Probably half way through the investigation itself. "Where? What're the details?"

"I'll tell you about it when Amanda's here. No use going over it twice," Dom paused. "You got more soda?"

"In the fridge."

Dom walked over to the kitchen, knowing he was torturing Brian. It was fun to make him crazy. This was going to be a great investigation for them. He stood in the white fluorescent light of the kitchen, taking his time opening the refrigerator door. Brian called over to him, "Where is it? At least tell me that."

"Centerville."

'Centerville? Centerville…why does that sound familiar?"

Dom let him think on it when there was another buzz to come up. Brian walked over to the intercom by the front door and punched the button. "Yo!" he yelled. "Where's your key?"

"In my bag, ass-hat. Let me in." He hit the button and buzzed her up.

"Centerville, huh?"

Dom nodded, grabbing a soda and letting the fridge door close on its own. He went back to the couch. Amanda walked in. She was a few years younger than Brian, but way ahead in maturity. An older soul, he'd say. Or she had that edge girls have over their brothers sometimes. She walked in like she owned the place, in gray shorts and a purple tank top, with dark sunglasses on top of her head. They kept her long brown hair at bay.

"Hey! I'm here. Let the party start," she smiled. Dom waved. He enjoyed having her around. She livened up a room, but when it was time to work, she was the first to get serious.

"Centerville! Hell, are you serious?" Brian paused. "Hey, Ammie."

She dropped her bag onto the dining room table and pulled up a chair. "Hey, Bri. What? What about Centerville? What did I miss?"

Dom smiled. "We got a request from a realtor to investigate a house he's trying to sell."

"In Centerville!" Brian added.

Amanda glanced from one to the other. "Centerville."

"Think, sis. Think!" Brian could hardly contain himself.

Her eyes got wide, the same way that Brian's had. They both had remarkably blue eyes, considering neither wore contacts. "Are you kidding?"

Dom shook his head. "Dead serious. Forgive the pun."

"The house with that murder…the one where they nailed the friend for it," she moved her hands in the air, as if that would help her remember. "The guy said it was some dark entity or something?"

"The one and only."

They all sat back, taking in what was before them. Dom began. "Jay, the realtor, wants either a 'yes, it's haunted' or a 'no, it's not,' as soon as possible. The house has been on the market but hasn't sold with its history. He says he gets calls from people who only want it if it's haunted and ones who will only touch it if it isn't."

Brian nodded. "I'd take it."

Amanda looked at him and rolled her eyes. "No, you wouldn't. Shut up."

"You know I would. In a heartbeat."

"Well, our work here is done," Amanda said. "Jay can sell it to Bri." Brian threw the remote at her leg. She jumped. "You missed." She turned to Dom. "When do we go in?

"We just have to name the date. He'll meet us and give us the keys."

She nodded. "What do we know already, beside that the guy was murdered?"

"He was a paranormal investigator, right?" Brian asked.

"Yeah. We know he kept a journal of his friend's supposed abuse. That came out in the trial. The buddy always contended that he was innocent…that some dark entity the guy had encountered was behind it all, even to the point of somehow transforming the journal. He said it had originally been the guy's paranormal diary or something. I guess there was a lot of activity in the house leading up to the murder. Supposed activity, anyway. It was pretty brutal."

"What about the guy himself? His history?" Amanda was in research mode. She was a great one to dive in, see what they had, and he knew when they left, she'd be on it all. Going deeper to get whatever might help them.

"I know he was a bus driver for one of the services up there," Brian added.

"We could interview his employer, maybe even some passengers."

"Nice. We should see what kind of history the house has. Who owned it before him, anything that might have happened in its past, tragedies, any deaths," Dom said.

"We should bring all of the equipment on this one. DVR, all cameras, meters, recorders… extra batteries." Brian said, going through his mental checklist. This was where he excelled. Dom knew if he had said 'Let's go,' Brian would be out the door.

"Yeah, we will. I want to gather as much information as we can before going in, but I want to get there as soon as possible."

"I'm off all this week," Amanda mentioned. "I can do some legwork and interview whoever I can find. Maybe we can get some info on the guy's mental state and see about that friend of his."

"Didn't he die recently? In prison? I think I read something about it."

"Yeah, I'm pretty sure he did. But was it murder or suicide? If it was suicide, well, that might point to some instability. Some weakness in his claims. But maybe we can get some info on him, too," Amanda had taken a yellow legal pad out of her oversized bag and was taking notes. "Centerville's what, like an hour-ish away?"

"Yeah, not bad at all," Dom responded. "I'm going to meet up with Jay and do a walkthrough with him, see what I can get out of him about the murder itself."

Brian smirked. "I can charge batteries."

Dom and Ammie laughed. "You can come with me, Big Brother," Amanda said. "Get off your ass, for once."

Dom grabbed his laptop case and took out the papers in the side pocket. He handed them to Brian and Amanda. "Some pictures I pulled off Zillow." The small white house sat at the dead end of Ridley Road, set back from the street. Unassuming. Pretty nearly a housewife's picket fence dream. Trees surrounded the yard behind the house and along its far side. It had a short driveway with a carport, side entryway. Pleasant enough. Friendly enough, if you didn't keep in mind that inside those walls some guy was beaten to death.

"Not a very big place," Brian commented.

"Nope. We should be able to cover it all with the cameras, then do some EVP sessions in the various rooms. We can concentrate where he was murdered and wherever there were reports of activity."

"Who claimed his things, after the murder? Did he have family?" Amanda was furiously taking notes, writing down questions they needed to answer and anything she could think of that would be relevant to their investigation. She tapped her pencil against her lips.

"Not sure, but it should be pretty easy to find out," Dom opened his laptop and set up on the dining room table. "We can at least do some internet searches to get a jumping off point."

They sat around the computer, giving Dom keywords to search. He punched in *Centerville murder* first. That brought up a number of articles about the house, including a few on a local murder from thirty years ago. Different place, unrelated, but it definitely showed what a small town Centerville was. The most exciting thing was the Halloween parade in 1979, shut down due to too much noise after 9 p.m. Brian smirked. "Someone'll probably call the cops on us, walking around that house after dark."

Dom clicked on the first article that popped up.

Houghton Bus Company driver and noted paranormal investigator, Jack Barnes, was murdered Sunday, November 8ᵗʰ, in his home. His longtime friend, Parker Davies, has been arrested for the crime. Barnes leaves behind a brother in Missouri. Funeral services are pending.

"Well," Amanda said. "We have his name, his employer, the date he was murdered, and his buddy's name. Even an ambiguous brother in the mix. Not a bad start, if I do say so myself."

Dom nodded. While he and Amanda continued brainstorming and running searches, Brian turned on his PC and hit the Renning County records office website to see if he could run ownership on the house. While it sat loading, he drummed his fingers on the table.

"You, the tech guy, with an outdated, old and slow computer held together with paperclips and spit," Dom said.

Brian smiled. "Ay, but she runs," he said. Amanda laughed at his overdone, trying to be Scottish, accent. It was reminiscent of Scotty from the old Star Trek series in a roundabout, not quite hitting the mark, way. "It seems the house itself was built in '53. Harriet and Nolan Browne built it and owned it till '72. They sold it to Roger and Mildred Parsons…" he read the listing, "and they sold it in '99 to Jack Barnes. That's our man. Not a huge history, should make checking things out pretty easy."

Amanda turned Dom's laptop to herself and started typing. She googled every name, every keyword she could think of to connect them to anything murderous, tragic, curious or unusual. Newspaper records, home ownership. Nothing. Public records searches. Marriages, births, deaths…all from old age or illness. Not one thing that would add to the paranormal history of the house that she could see. Brian started trying to find any events tied to the property itself. 11 Ridley Road. Nothing. Every search he did, he came up empty-handed. It seemed to be a quiet little house on a dead-end road in a sleepy little town. Boring as hell, but it made this murder more notable. At least to him.

"Aren't the quiet spots the ones with the deepest, darkest secrets? Don't they usually have the sickest histories?" Brian stated more than asked. "That's how Stephen King would write it."

Dom leaned back in his chair. It was satisfying to work with people who could take initiative, even if Brian could be a little "over enthusiastic" at times. He grabbed a notepad out of his laptop case and started working on questions to ask the realtor.

"I'll tell you, I'm learning more about Centerville than I ever needed to know," Brian said, intrigued but exasperated. He tapped his fingers on his keyboard as if willing them to come up with something on their own. "This sleepy little town is a snore."

Dom laughed. "Yeah, for sure."

"What about court transcripts?" Amanda asked. "If the trial is public record, shouldn't we be able to get ahold of the transcripts?"

"I hadn't thought of that. Seems reasonable. I don't know if there's a waiting period before they're released or what the procedure is to get them, but definitely something we should check out."

Amanda made another note on her pad and tucked her hair behind her left ear. It was a cute habit she had and Dom let it go at that. Amanda was like a sister to him, and Brian the little brother you loved but wanted to punch sometimes. It was by accident that they found each other. His previous team had broken apart, "irreconcilable differences," and he was putting up a flyer at the local library. He and Brian literally bumped into each other as he put the sign on the cork board and, with Brian's enthusiasm for the paranormal, he had to bring him on. At least temporarily. When Brian told him that his sister was also interested in joining a team and that she was sensitive to paranormal "things," it all fell into place. The rest was history, as they say. Although he could've kept investigating on his own, he knew better. It was the first rule of being a ghost hunter…never go out in the field alone. Common sense, really. If you got hurt, fell down a well or were attacked by who knows what, you needed at the very least another person who could help. Call 911. Something. In his opinion, the minimum should be four. Two at base camp and two going through the site, rotating at intervals. Once in while they had a fourth friend along but his team was a pretty solid three.

"When are you meeting with the realtor?" Brian asked, spinning around in his chair. "When do you think we can go in?"

"I've got an appointment at 5 p.m. tomorrow." He was glad it was summer and he could easily fit in this investigation. Dom taught at the local community college during the school year but took summers off. It was the nice thing about teaching; it left him free enough to follow his paranormal passion. He'd toyed with the idea of approaching the college about teaching a summer evening program on ghost hunting, or a winter "ghost course." It'd be a few extra dollars in his pocket, and he'd enjoy it. Not that he didn't like his course load now; he loved bringing literature to the kids, but there was something a bit more "alive" about the dead. Ah, well. It paid the bills. And he still had a week before classes started. "I'll set it up the earliest we can get it. When are you free? He's pretty eager."

"Maybe one night this week? My schedule's open."

"Your schedule is always open," Amanda chimed in. "Get a job, loser." She threw her pencil at her brother. He smiled at her and tossed it onto her notepad. "I'll fit in whatever night works for you guys. I can grab some extra coffee and deal at work, if need be. Tomorrow I'm free and I can take a ride to the bus station, see what information I can track down."

"Sounds like a plan. I think we've got this rolling now," Dom started packing up his laptop, the photos. "After I meet with Jay, I'll let you know what I've found out and when we're in. We'll work out any extra details then."

Brian nodded, going to the fridge for another Coke. "Yeah, man. Can't wait." Dom left. He was pretty damned excited, too.

2

Joe signed the release forms at the hospital. Great. A fucking concussion and a bruised back. Be worse tomorrow, most likely. X-rays, waiting, doctors, waiting. He wondered what it would've been like if he'd been dying. Nothing was a priority in the emergency room, that was sure. He watched the second hand of the clock on the wall. Tick tick tick. Finally, the doctor came in with his results and told him he'd probably miss a week of work, depending. He'd need to watch his symptoms. He should've known better, should've been more careful. Yeah, yeah. He was pissed as hell he went up that ladder and now he'd be out of commission because of it.

It had been a gorgeous morning, too nice to stay inside, and he was trying to adjust the satellite dish on his roof. The apartment's roof. Whatever. Nothing had been going right for him lately and he was damn sick of it all. All he had wanted to do was fix the dish, do a little outdoor work and relax before Monday came along bringing the usual bullshit. He'd brought the ladder out of the storeroom and leaned it against the brick building. Even checked the feet, made sure they were stable and set into the ground before heading up. Nothing new to someone who'd been in construction all his life.

He stepped onto the ladder, testing it, swaying his weight a little, and moved up the first few rungs. As he got higher, he passed a kitchen window and glanced in. The dark mass coalesced faster than his mind could comprehend. Most of the window was obscured and he felt cold air rush past his legs. It circled him and shoved. How can air fucking push you? How can a shadow do anything? It didn't make any sense but, as he fell, grabbing at the ladder as he went, he was sure he saw a dark face in that window. Grinning. He'd twisted his back trying to catch himself, to break his fall, and bounced onto the ground. Imbedded in the dirt was a rock just waiting to crack his skull. Figures. He guessed it could've been a lot worse. There was blood all over his shirt, but head wounds bleed. A lot. He learned that years ago. He'd been at camp the first time he'd split his head open. The counselor was crabby after watching fifteen 10-year olds all day in the summer heat and told them to each get a rock from the field to throw into the woods. Naturally they had all run out to the field to find the biggest rocks. A boy he hardly knew, a big beefy kid with man-boobs already in the making, wailed one from about twelve feet behind him. His aim sucked or Joe turned at the wrong time and SLAP, the next thing he knew he had staff crowded around, a bandage covering his temple and blood flowing down his face.

He could still hear his father yelling into the phone and how it made his head hurt. That counselor didn't finish out the season, his bags were packed before Joe returned from the ER. That was his first experience with being an inconvenient emergency. He put his hand up to the bandage covering his wound and winced.

"Have you got someone to drive you home?"

"I'm sorry, what?" he was snapped out of his thoughts.

"Have you got someone to drive you home?" the nurse with his paperwork asked. She was somewhat heavyset, with the longest painted nails he'd ever seen. He wondered how she wiped her ass with those.

"Oh, yeah, no. I can get a cab," he informed her, stuffing his insurance card back into his wallet. It wasn't even a lie since one of the painters had called the ambulance for him. His truck would be sitting in the apartment lot. Shit. That'd be one more bill coming. He hadn't needed an ambulance. Unreal. Should make the painter pay it.

He walked outside into the sunshine and sat on a bench to wait for the taxi. The sun felt great on his skin and there was a light breeze blowing. He stared at the hospital landscape; neat little trees and bushes lined the parking lot, hills in the background. Marigolds and petunias edged the walkway in huge terra cotta pots. "Your healthcare dollars at work, folks," he muttered. The cars rolled in, up to the front, out to the parking spaces, with a continuous flow of people in and out. He checked his watch, lit a cigarette, and fielded the dirty looks of those who went by. Fuck them. If he wanted to kill himself one breath at a time, that was his business. His mind drifted to the accident and he shivered despite the summer sun.

It had to be a coincidence, but everything started going downhill after he began using that board. The board. Huh. Spirit board, Ouija board. What the hell was a Ouija anyway? All he had wanted was to mess around with it, see if it worked. Yeah. That was a joke. It worked like a son of a bitch and now, well. His fall couldn't be from that. He had to be imagining it, talking himself scared. He started counting up issues, everything that he'd screwed up in the last few weeks. Rita was the biggest. Their relationship. Hah! That was gone. He shook his head, as if he could throw off the thought and not have to feel the loss. Joe flicked the end of his cigarette and took another lungful of smoke, watching the ashes hit the ground. When you go into a rage and nearly beat the hell out of a woman…he sighed. She was right to leave. He'd never hit a woman before in his life. Ever. The rage came out of nowhere. He didn't understand it and hoped he never would. He rubbed his hand along the outside of his thigh.

His truck had died, too. The next day. Absolutely fucking died in the middle of traffic, for no good reason. Not only did he have cars honking their horns at him, he had to roll the damn thing off the road. The mechanic checked it, this was wrong, that was wrong… all small things. Nothing that should have killed it like that. Try this, try that. At least it was working. For now. And the bank! He exhaled.

For some reason, the bank had decided that he hadn't paid on his mortgage in the last eight months. What the hell? He made his payments. Sometimes they were a little late. Well, sometimes a lot late, but he still made them. Something was screwed up in their paper work. Someone had entered something wrong into their computer. He didn't know. But whoever it was, they must be civil servants working for the universe that hated him. There was no record of any of his checks clearing his bank, either. He took another drag, blew out a smoke ring and watched it dissipate. To hell with it. They could have the house. He already had all his things moved into the manager's apartment at Forest View. But he couldn't shake the feeling that something was against him and he wasn't sure what.

The taxi pulled around the loop in front of the hospital and stopped. Joe gently eased himself into the passenger seat. "Forest View, and please, avoid the fucking potholes." He managed a weak smile at the driver in the knit beanie beside him. The guy nodded, putting the car into gear. He thumbed through his paperwork as they drove, one hand out the window, trying to keep the cigarette behind the side mirror, buffered from the wind.

It only took about fifteen minutes to get home. He paid the beanie guy and slowly walked to the entrance. The main door was open. He'd be damn lucky if the place hadn't been cleaned out. No thanks to the crew working there. He drew a last hit off his cigarette and flicked it onto the pavement. Rolling his eyes, he bent over and scooped the butt up. Painfully. Can't have the grounds messy. He rubbed his eyes and walked in, letting the entry doors close and lock behind him, and took the "West Staircase." Yeah, that was fancy for "This Way to the Basement." He didn't care, his recliner and a cold beer were waiting. Oh, wait. The words "NO ALCOHOL" stood out on his paperwork. Damn it. The universe interfering again. He unlocked his office door, the ex-morgue door, and went in. There was no way he was going to do any work today. He swung open the door that joined the office to his apartment, sat down and picked up the remote. Out of habit he clicked it on, and remembered the ladder. Fuck. He hadn't found the satellite's problem and now he was stuck in the house with no TV. And he wouldn't be going up on that ladder anytime soon. As he muttered, the television came to life. With picture. What the hell. He flipped through the channels. Well, maybe the satellite company flipped a switch, found a glitch, who knew. At least it was on. He set the alarm on his phone for 6:30 p.m. The doc told him to sleep for only two hours at a time the first night, in case it was worse than they thought. Call if there's confusion; is there anyone who can stay with you? Please. Listening to some reality show crap, he drifted off.

3

Amanda called Brian from her apartment first thing Monday morning. "Hey, you gonna come with me today?" She could hear him fumbling with the phone and he dropped it at least twice.

"Wha? What time is it?"

"8:30, lazy ass. Are you going to come with me or what?"

"Nah, Ammie, I want to get everything charged up. I don't like to leave with batteries plugged in, know what I mean? I want to make sure it's set when Dom gives us the go time."

"Yeah, I get it. Not a problem, big bro."

"Love ya. Next time wait an extra hour before calling."

"Yeah, yeah. I'll call you later," she said and dropped her phone onto the bed. She finished toweling off her hair and grabbed her black tee from the drawer. *Out of the Dark Paranormal* was in small print on the pocket. She tucked the shirt into her jeans and checked herself out in the mirror over her dresser. Cute, but not her favorite look on a hot summer day. The outdoor thermometer already read 75 degrees. She'd be representing her team, though, and that she took seriously. She pulled her hair up into a ponytail.

Glancing around the room, she felt the "I haven't picked up in far too long" guilt. Socks, a tee shirt and a few pairs of jeans were strewn here and there. They were clean, but deposited wherever she dropped them when she decided they weren't what she wanted to wear that day. "Hmm, maybe when I get back," she said. Most likely, she'd put them all into the clean clothes basket and they'd stay there till she pawed through them once again. Her living room was cluttered as well, but not dirty. Lived in. That's what it was, she thought. Lived in.

"My phone, my phone," she said under her breath, searching her sofa before remembering it was on her bed. She dug in her purse for her car keys, took a clipboard and notepad, and stepped into the hallway, tripping over a pair of shoes she had left by the door. "Damn it!" She caught herself before she could fall.

Her neighbor, Mrs. Winters, was in the hallway. "Morning, dear. Be careful."

Amanda gathered herself and thanked her. She went quickly and happily down the side steps and out into the parking lot. Her car, a yellow 2012 VW bug, was waiting. "Hiya, Vinnie. We're going on an adventure today." She gave it a tap on the hood. For some reason, every car had a name to her and VW Vinnie felt right. In bad weather he was Vincent, and she could always depend on him.

She tossed her things on the passenger seat and googled the address of Jack Barnes' employer. *Houghton Bus Service, 134 Midtown Avenue.* She typed it into her GPS and turned the key in the VW's ignition. "Let's do this, Vin. Sixty-five miles ahead of us."

She picked up the highway at the edge of town. Probably fifty-seven miles were straight highway, long and boring. As she drove, she had the windows down, but the heat today was pushing her limit. At least Vinnie had air conditioning. She hit the blower to low and left the windows cracked. Even with the cool recycled air in her face, she loved the fresh coming in.

Amanda watched the trees go by, green exit signs for the different towns here and there, and wished she lived closer to Centerville. Her excitement was growing as she drove. How amazing that they would be investigating the Barnes house. Everyone had heard about the murder when it happened. It caught all the papers and local television news channels. She remembered it being described as horrific. It was even worse that his closest friend had supposedly done it. The guy swore he was innocent throughout the entire trial, maintaining that some evil force had moved in, attacked his friend and finally killed him. The media had a field day calling it the "Dark Entity Defense." She felt terrible for the guy… Parker, she thought. If he hadn't done it, his life and reputation were destroyed. If he had, well…then he was a sick bastard.

"The Barnes house," she said. She was proud that she'd be on the team going in. Her GPS let her know that in two miles she'd be taking exit 112 into Centerville and she was thrilled to see that there was a Dunkin Donuts sign. She had run out of the house without breakfast and was getting hungry.

As she slowed off the exit and merged into traffic, she could see the DD sign in the distance. She wondered if Jack Barnes had ever gone to that particular coffee house. Had he waited on the drive through line just as she would? Asked for a medium hot coffee, milk and sugar? She got a bagel with cream cheese and her coffee and parked, watching the cars drive by. People watching was a favorite of hers. She wanted to know everyone's backstory. Where were they coming from, what was their motivation, where were they going? Maybe that's why she enjoyed researching so much. She loved figuring out the historical background of the sites they visited, the names, the lives. It fascinated her.

A Houghton bus went by, pulling into a bus stop that must've been for the strip mall down the street. That might have been HIS bus. Maybe it was his route. She savored her bagel and coffee, watching and wondering.

Amanda shook the crumbs from her lap and stuffed the bagel wrapper into the coffee cup in the cup holder. It sat next to another empty cup, and there was a bag of fast food napkins and containers from the other day sitting on the passenger floor mat. She probably should have thrown them out in the bin at the drive-thru but hadn't. Clutter, again. She'd get to it, though. Soon. She turned the key and backed out of her parking space. If she trusted her GPS, and she did, she'd be at Houghton in less than five minutes. Three, if traffic was light.

She traveled on about a mile and could see the station ahead. The light turned red and she stopped, checking her face in the mirror. Couldn't walk in with bits of bagel in her teeth or her lipstick smeared. All was well and she continued on when it flipped to green. She turned in and parked, going over and over in her mind the best approach to Barnes' employer. "Hi, I'm from a paranormal team investigating the house of your dead employee, what can you tell me?" would not be the way to go. She smiled, trying to think of something that would be a little gentler but would yield the results she was looking for. She slipped her purse over her shoulder, tucked her clipboard under her arm and walked purposefully into the station.

A middle-aged man sat at the only desk in the small office. There were a couple of folding tables and a coffee pot cooking the hell out of the morning's coffee behind him. Beside it sat a leaning tower of Styrofoam cups, sugar packets and a carton of who-knew-how-old milk. Sporting a bit of a beer belly and a comb over that needed to be combed over, the man had on a Houghton shirt and was rearranging piles of paperwork in front of him. Rings of coffee stains coated the old desk.

"Can I help you?" he asked.

"I hope so," she said. She held out her hand to shake his. "Amanda Harper. I'm doing some historical research on a house owned by one of your former employees and I was wondering if you could give me some information on him?"

"Earl Haines," he told her. He shook her hand, then leaned back in his office chair. It bounced a little and she thought it might snap leaving her to call 911. She was relieved that he was well versed in its rocking, though, and balanced like one of the Flying Walldendas. "I run this place. I'm not quite sure what type of info you're looking for. I don't give out anything personal about my guys. You should probably talk to the person directly."

"Well, it's on Jack Barnes."

Earl sat bolt upright and his face went serious. "You're a reporter. I thought all that was done years ago. I ain't got nothing more to say on that matter." He stared intently at his papers and pretended to be searching through them for something that needed his immediate attention. He slid an overflowing ash tray out of his way.

Amanda stood for a moment considering the situation. Quietly she said, "I'm not a reporter, Mr. Haines. I am actually trying to get a feel for the man himself. His personality. I belong to a paranormal team that's been asked to go in and investigate his home." She reached into her purse and handed him one of Out of the Dark's business cards. "We mean no disrespect. We're only trying to understand the man a little before we go in."

Earl sat back again, less far this time, and looked at Amanda, sizing her up. "One of them ghost hunters, eh?"

She nodded.

"Like on TV? This isn't going to be on TV, is it?"

"No, sir. This is just to document if there is or isn't anything paranormal going on. I'm gathering the history of the house, previous owners, the tragedy and everything I can ahead of time. It helps us to focus our investigation. Anything we find will be kept confidential."

Earl sat, thinking about what she said. "I watch some of those ghost shows."

She smiled. "I do, too."

"Ever been at the old house on Mason Avenue?"

She shook her head.

"That's an old one. Probably has some activity because it's so old. You should try there."

"Mason?" Amanda asked, grabbing her pencil and making a note. "Perhaps sometime we will."

Earl nodded with a slight smile and stood. He hobbled over to a folding chair resting on the wall behind his desk. It looked as old and stained as the coffee pot, and he opened it up next to his seat. "Come sit and we'll talk."

Amanda eagerly sat, her clipboard in her lap.

Earl eased himself down. "These old knees," he looked at her. "It's hell to get old." He took a deep breath and let it out slowly. "What did you want to know about Jack?"

"Truly, anything you can tell me. What was he like? Was he happy, friendly, a loner…"

"Ah, Jack. He was okay. A good guy. Responsible. I think in all the years he worked here, he was only late once or twice. Liked to joke. He was big on puns." Earl paused, remembering. "Awful what happened. Damned tragic."

"Yes. I'm so sorry for your loss."

He nodded. "Time has helped some, but not entirely. Who knew? No one saw it coming."

"Were you good friends?"

"Acquaintances, really. We only interacted here, but we had a great work relationship."

"Was he married? Have a girlfriend? Any other friends besides…"

"The rat that killed him?"

Amanda paused. "Yes."

"He was divorced. A long time ago, I think. No kids that I know of. He had just started dating a girl not long before he died."

"Oh? Do you know her name?" she continued to take notes as he talked.

Earl thought for a minute. "I don't think he ever said. She was local, though. A waitress, I think, over at A Touch of Home. Not sure if she's still there. Years change things and if I were her, I would've moved after it all. Too many reporters sticking their noses into things. Makes life uncomfortable." He touched her shoulder. "Not you, dear."

She smiled. Earl was a sweet man. She could tell he cared about

Jack. "How does it work here? Did Jack work with other drivers? Share routes?"

"Jack knew the couple of other drivers that we had. He had one bus, his own route. He would switch off with another guy. Bill. You know, if one was out sick or on vacation, the other knew the route and would take it. We would rotate a different driver into Bill's spot, kind of like a circular rotation, if that makes any sense. It was Bill that switched with Jack. Yeah. But talking to him won't give you much. They weren't friends outside of work. Bill drives Jack's route now."

Amanda was furiously writing on her yellow pad. "Bill? Would I be able to ride along on his route, just to see it...get a feel for it? Maybe talk to a passenger or two?"

"Hmm... you'd definitely be able to ride it. I don't know if I'd say to go talking to the passengers. That might not be met well. He had a few regulars, but that doesn't mean they'd want to chat."

"I understand. I wouldn't bother anyone," she said. She met his gaze, "I promise."

Earl gave a quick smile. "I like you. Yeah, you can ride his route. I'll even let you get on for free." He slapped the desk to punctuate the thought.

"Thank you! How nice."

"Is there anything else you'd like to know?"

She thought for a moment. "Were there any changes in him toward the end? His personality, his routine?"

"Not that I can think of... except, there were a few days he came in looking really tired, but that might've been a late date the night before," he winked. "He missed about a week of work right before he was killed. The flu, I think. Probably not what you're looking for, but it was unusual in a guy who was never absent." He checked his watch. "Bill should be in in about fifteen minutes. Just before he starts his afternoon run he comes in to pick up any route changes. If you have the time, you could go with him."

"That'd be great. Thank you so much." Amanda picked up her

clipboard and purse. She held out her hand to shake Earl's. "I do appreciate you taking the time to talk to me."

"I hope I helped, even a little. And I hope you find whatever might need finding. He was a good man. He didn't deserve what he got."

She nodded and walked out from behind Earl's desk. She stood in the hallway, looking at the corkboard postings while waiting for Bill to come in. Job offerings, kids' school fundraisers, buy it/sell its. After a short wait, a man walked in wearing a dark green painter's cap. He stopped at Earl's desk. "Hot today. Good thing that air conditioner's fixed or I'd be quitting," he said.

"Yeah, it's a boiler for sure," Earl answered. "Bill, that little lady over there," he pointed in Amanda's direction. "Take her with you on your run. No fee."

Bill looked at Amanda, then eyed his boss. "Okay."

"For Jack."

Bill's eyes got wide and he raised an eyebrow. "Okay."

Earl nodded, brushing him off. "She'll tell you about it. It's fine. She's not a reporter."

Bill took his papers and walked over to Amanda. "Guess you're with me."

"Great," she said. "I'm Amanda. Nice to meet you," she offered as they walked out of the glass door to the station. The sun and heat hit them as they stepped outside. "Wow!" Amanda pulled her shades off the top of her head and shielded her eyes.

"Pretty darned hot out here," Bill stated. "That's our ride." His bus was parked beside the building, big and blue with "Houghton" on the side. The door was open and he climbed into the driver's seat. She went up the steps and took one of the seats directly behind him.

"So," he paused, closing the bus doors and starting the engine. "You knew Jack?"

"Oh, no," she shook her head. "I'm doing some research. I'm with a team that's been asked to come in to check out his house."

He raised an eyebrow. "What type of team?"

She paused. "Paranormal."

"Is that usual with house sales now?" he asked while he waited for a break in the traffic. He eased onto the main road.

"No, not really," she watched his expression in the rear mirror over the windshield, trying to decide if he was believing her or thinking she was nuts. It was about 50/50 with the people she met. Either they were wholeheartedly into ghosts and things that went bump in the night or they regarded her suspiciously, as if she were a snake-oil salesman.

"I see."

"I was researching the owners of the house, its history. I'm trying to get a feel for the most recent owner before we go in."

"Have there been…things…going on there? Probably should be with what happened. You know what his friend said, too, I'm sure."

"I haven't heard reports of any activity. His friend…"

"The one they arrested," Bill watched the cars for a moment, then switched lanes. "Parker Davies. He said it was some evil thing in the house."

"Yeah. I heard that."

"Do you think it was? Something evil?"

"I don't know."

Bill drove along in a somewhat uncomfortable silence.

"Did you know Jack well?" Amanda asked.

"Well enough, I guess. Nice guy. Liked to kid around. That's about it."

Amanda watched out the window, taking note of the stops they made, the people that got on and off. She discreetly scrutinized each one, the way they interacted with Bill. Did they seem like regulars? Or just shoppers, people headed to the medical facility…or newcomers who wouldn't have known Jack? He'd been gone now… three or four years? She considered everything like the paranormal detective she considered herself.

Disappointment crept in as time went by. She had thought this was a great idea but so far the only information she had gotten was from Earl, and the bus ride was turning out to be exactly that. A bus ride. She sighed and stared out the window, watching Main Street flow along. When Bill swung past the college for the third time, Amanda decided it was her last circle around the town. She'd already spent the afternoon people watching, and no one seemed approachable. Tucking her clipboard into her purse, she resigned herself to a day spent with good intentions that didn't pan out. It happened all the time in the paranormal field. Ah, well.

Bill brought the bus to a stop at the medical facility. Inside a little rain enclosure was a short, elderly woman in an enormous hat. Little flowers covered its brim, in all the colors of a summer garden. Reds, yellows, purples, greens. She adjusted it and carefully made her way toward them. Bill waited. The old woman reached up to hold onto the railing. Amanda went down the steps and took her other arm.

"Why, thank you, dear."

The woman took the first seat behind the driver and beside Amanda. Once she was settled, Bill closed the bus doors and continued on.

"You're quite welcome."

"It's my knees, you know. Shoulder's sore today, too, but the doctor doesn't want to hear it."

"I see," Amanda responded.

"I'm Mabel. Mabel Trumbel. Awful name, isn't it? Never liked it. Doesn't flow." Mabel looked out the windows on the opposite wall of the bus.

"Oh, no," Amanda said. "I quite like it. My name's Amanda Harper. It's very nice to meet you, Mrs. Trumbel."

Mabel gave her a slight smile. "Call me Mabel, Amanda."

"Alright, Mabel. Thank you. Lovely day, minus the heat."

"I don't mind the heat so much," Mabel responded. "It means I only wear two sweaters instead of three!" She broke out in a chuckle that only someone pushing ninety could do.

Amanda thought she was quite adorable. She laughed.

"Now tell me, dear Amanda," Mabel paused. "Are you new to this hum drum town? I haven't seen you on the bus before."

"Oh, no. I'm just visiting for the day."

"Ah. Visiting? Well, there's not a lot to visit here…and if it were family related, you wouldn't be sitting on this little bus riding through town, now would you? Curious." Mabel turned to look out the other windows. She didn't like to miss the street signs or window displays as they went through the main part of town. "So, what is this visit, if you don't mind me asking?"

"I'm doing some research, actually. For my team," she took her clipboard from her purse.

"Research… Team," Mabel paused, considering what Amanda had said. She looked her straight in the eye. "You're can feel them, can't you?"

"Excuse me?"

"The spirits. I know you do. I do, too, sweetie. Nothing to be embarrassed about." Mabel had a self-satisfied little smile on her face. She adjusted her flower hat.

"Oh, I'm not embarrassed. Really."

Mabel patted her hand.

"My team is doing research on a house in town."

Mabel looked at her out of the corner of her eye and sat, not saying anything, hands resting on her clip-top purse. Its floral design didn't quite match her hat.

"Jack Barnes' house…" Amanda started.

"I know," Mabel cut her off before she could continue the sentence. "I knew Jack."

Amanda perked up. "Would you be willing to tell me about him? What he was like?" She took the pencil from under the clip and positioned it, ready to take down anything Mabel could offer.

"What do you really want to know, Amanda?"

"Well, I…"

"He wasn't crazy." Mabel stared ahead, watching the cars. "He was a good man. Loved his cat." She tapped Amanda's clipboard with her well-manicured nails. "Write that down, too, dear."

Amanda added "loved his cat" to the list of Jack's attributes.

"He also did the ghost hunting. Like you. Liked to find reasons for things," she turned back to Amanda. "There aren't always reasons. Or at least the ones he wanted to find." She leaned in closer, her voice lower. "I warned him."

"Warned him? Against…?" Amanda half-whispered.

"He got involved with something dark. I could feel it all around him. I told him to be careful." She sat leaning to see more clearly around Bill. "Hard to get away from that sometimes. Tragic." She shook her head.

"So you don't believe it was his friend, then?"

"My dear, I know it wasn't," she gathered herself and, as Bill pulled the bus to a slow stop, she stood. "This is my stop, Amanda. It was nice talking to you." Adjusting her hat, she went tentatively down the steps.

"Thank you, Mabel," Amanda called after her. The little old woman waved with her free arm, the other clutching her purse. She was met by someone she knew who walked with her toward the senior apartments.

Amanda absently tapped her pencil on her notepad. Not crazy. Warned him. Something dark. Now this was getting interesting. She rode with Bill until they returned to the bus company, then ran in to thank Earl once more for letting her ride along. You always caught more flies with honey than with vinegar and she truly did appreciate his generosity. She glanced at the clock in the hallway before leaving. 2:15 p.m. Not bad. She'd be home by 3:30 and be able to chat with Dom and Brian before Dom's walkthrough of the house. She made her way to VW Vinnie in the lot. "Ugh, Vin," she complained, opening the car doors and tossing her things onto the passenger seat.

The heat poured out in waves. She stood outside, checking her messages while she waited for the car to de-swelter. There were a few emails from Dom, articles from the trial. She'd read them when she got home.

As she drove back to Hilldale, her mind spun on what Mabel had said. What dark thing could Barnes have become involved with? Had he been into Satan worship? Black masses? He was a paranormal investigator in his own right, did he find something on a site? Have some sort of negative attachment? Mabel meant it when she said he wasn't crazy, and she seemed well in control of her faculties.

Barnes' friend, Parker something, had said it was an entity, too. Now, she couldn't wait to get home and go over the articles Dom had found. Print them out, pour over them for some clue to whatever had gone on with Jack Barnes. See if there was any correlation between what Parker had maintained and Mabel had mentioned. The miles rolled out behind her the more she turned everything over in her mind.

Amanda parked Vinnie in his usual spot, grabbed her purse and clipboard off the passenger seat and headed inside. She took the stairs two by two, excited to be back, and circled into her hallway to find Brian sitting cross legged in front of her apartment door. He was flipping through pics on his phone, looking thoroughly bored.

"What are you doing here?" she asked, stepping over him to unlock the door.

"Thought I'd come by, see what you found out. Dom sent some interesting emails about the trial and I was curious."

"You get everything charged?"

"Yeah," he said, standing up and stretching. "Most of it just needed to be topped off. Everything else I'll pop in fresh batteries. Stopped at the store and reloaded our supply." He followed her into the apartment, looking around. "I need to get a key. Haven't picked up in a while, I see."

"It's lived in, Bri. Deal."

He sat on her couch, moving a pile of clothes to the recliner.

"At least they're folded, right?" she smiled at him. "How long were you waiting?"

"About half an hour."

"You're a goof."

"I prefer quirky," he put his feet up on her couch.

"Hey… shoes off. I may be cluttered but I'm not dirty."

"All right, all right," he kicked off his shoes. "What did you find out?"

"Well…everyone liked Barnes, but his coworkers didn't know him very well."

"Not unusual," Brian stated.

"True," Amanda sat down, giving Brian's feet a shove out of her way. "I also rode his bus route, checked out the passengers and the area."

"And?"

"I met one little old lady who used to ride with him. She seemed to have a pretty good feel for him. Sensitive, too."

Brian raised an eyebrow. "Oh?" He had lived with his sister's sensitivities growing up, and in their investigations it sometimes helped…gave them a more focused direction to head in. Sometimes.

"Yeah. She felt he wasn't crazy at all…and that his friend wasn't the one who killed him."

"Who did she think did it?"

"Something dark. She said she felt it around him and warned him to be careful."

"Interesting. Wow."

"Right? I thought the next step would be to go through what Dom sent to see if we could find any parallels."

"Get printing, Sis. Let's do this."

Amanda opened each email in her phone, there were three or four, and sent them to her printer. While it got to work churning out pages, she went into the kitchen. "Have you had lunch?"

"Are you kidding? I'm starved!"

She smiled. Typical Brian. "I've got some sandwich stuff, if you want…"

Before she could finish her sentence, he was reaching past her to get the rolls and mustard. "Thanks, Ammie." He flashed a grin that made her give in. He had always been the pain in the neck big brother with a disarming charm.

She brought out sliced turkey and provolone, placing them on the counter. "Oil and vinegar or mayo?"

"Oil and vinegar, Sis. Always o and v."

Another smile. Even growing up he had had an aversion to mayonnaise. Never a problem with potato salad or coleslaw but, as soon as it came near bread of any kind, he was disgusted. Odd kid. She reached into the refrigerator and brought out the vinegar. "The oil's up in the cabinet."

"Already have it." He had taken over her kitchen, slicing tomatoes, ripping lettuce leaves and building the "ultimate" sandwich.

"I hope you're slicing some of that for me."

"I cut too much," he paused. "I mean, yeah, of course I did."

Amanda gave him a shove.

"Hey! Never push the man with the knife."

They got their sandwiches plated and brought them into the living room to the coffee table. Amanda pulled the papers from the printer and sat down while Brian went into the kitchen for some iced tea.

"Ice?"

"Of course! It's summer."

He handed her a wonderfully chilly glass of tea and sat beside her. They put the stack of papers between them and read while they ate.

Willow Tree Weekly, October 24, 2016

As Halloween quickly approaches, we'd like to remind our readers to stay safe and stay away from the New Castle Asylum grounds. Even though the abandoned institution has long been rumored to be haunted, and figured prominently in the murder trial of Parker Davies, it is in remarkable disrepair and could prove to be quite dangerous to anyone walking through. Our local sheriff's office has advised that they will be patrolling the area with the safety of all in mind.

Amanda put her sandwich on her plate and got her notepad. "New Castle? New Castle. What's that got to do with it all?" She jotted down the name. "Where is Willow Tree Weekly even out of?"

Brian grabbed his phone and started searching. "Fremont. New Castle is in Freemont, along with Willow Tree Weekly."

"It was an asylum?"

"Here, look," Brian handed her his phone so she could scroll through photos of the institution…from when it was new to later when it sat abandoned.

"Creepy place. I wonder what it has to do with Parker, Jack and the murder."

"Turn the page," Brian suggested. "Maybe we'll find out." He took another bite of his sandwich while she went to the next article. They read for what was left of the afternoon.

4

Never an early riser, Joe opened one eye and saw it was 10:30 a.m. Sheesh. He closed his eyes and tried to sink deeper into his pillows. His concussion wasn't having it. Fuck. It'd been more than two weeks since his injury and he still had a dull ache in his head. Not only did he want to stay in bed, he had absolutely no desire to get up and work. That wouldn't sit well with his bosses, though, or his paycheck. He forced himself into a sitting position. The room spun but at least the nausea was gone.

Joe sighed and stood, steadying himself on the wall beside his bed. He rested his head against the cool plaster until it eased up. As badly as he needed to pee, he took his time walking into the bathroom, not wanting to stir up the brain demons any more than they already were. He freed his dick from his pajama pants and exhaled as his pee streamed into the toilet. "Almost better than sex," he muttered, and turned to start the shower. Damn, he wanted a bath, but since his concussion he hated getting in and out of the tub. If the dizziness kicked in, he figured he'd drown himself trying to stand up. Hopefully all this shit would fix itself soon. He wondered how NFL players could be cleared to be on the field a week or two after a big hit. Shit. If they paid him $32 million, he'd be out there even if he was puking up his guts. But they don't. For his salary, they could wait till afternoon. That's why they made voicemail, right?

The bathroom started to fill with steam; the fresh pale blue paint job looking shiny with condensation. Or maybe it was his eyes. He gingerly stepped over the side of the tub, feeling like a fucking old woman advertising a necklace clicker. "I've fallen and I can't get up." Hell no. He grabbed the handshower and aimed it at his back. It felt great. He stood there a while letting it wash over his muscles. Weird. He could almost feel the individual drops. And not like water drops. It was as if they were hitting harder, like little slaps and smacks. With precision. He turned quickly and recoiled, letting the metal hose fall and clang into the wall. What the actual fuck?!

Maggots. Bugs. Not climbing out of the handshower, but *flowing*. Like the water. They *were* the water. He jumped around, swiping at his back, trying to make sure nothing was on him, *crawling* on him, and scrambled out of the tub. He was bent over, head pounding and breathing hard, when he turned around.

Water was pouring across the wall tile and into the tub. Down the drain. Easily. Not clogged with bugs. Nothing swirling in the water. Not even a fly in the room. He rubbed his eyes and shivered, standing on the bathmat, dripping. No bugs. What the hell was wrong with him? Could a concussion bring hallucinations? He didn't want to have to call the doc again. But maybe there was something wrong with him. Maybe he was losing his mind. Joe looked again at the water. He was done. At least he'd rinsed off, right? He reached over and turned off the faucet. Grabbing a towel from the rack, he dried off, checking his back in the mirror. He'd feel crawly the rest of the day. Another shiver. God, he hated bugs.

Joe pulled the frying pan from the drawer under his oven and set it on the stove. Some scrambled eggs and he'd feel better. Yeah, right. He couldn't get the feeling of the bugs out of his skin. It had to be all in his fucking mind, but damn. He cracked two eggs and stirred them quickly with some milk in the pan. Yeah, that's what his brain felt like. Scrambled eggs. Next time he'd leave the satellite adjustments to the pros. Fuck it. TV wasn't worth this.

The eggs sizzled and he threw a slice of American cheese over the top to melt while he mixed some instant coffee with tap water. He hadn't let the water run long enough to get hot and now what he had was a lukewarm swirling mass of half melted crystals. Damn it. This wasn't going to be his day. He made a face and chugged the cup, grimacing with the bitter aftertaste. Caffeine was caffeine, and he was going to need it today. He scraped the eggs out of the pan and tossed it into the sink to soak. Yeah, maybe he'd feel more like himself after he ate. Anything would be better than that coffee.

Joe checked his phone for the weather report. Hot and sunny. Again. What he wouldn't give for some rain. The greenhouse had delivered some shrubs and flowers that he ordered and he'd be putting them in in the heat. He could've had them plant it all, but the owners had landscaping monies in his budget. Why should he pay it out to someone else? He could get these bushes and things in, beautify the damn place, and pay himself. Why the fuck not? It wasn't as if he had any tenants to watch over yet. All the preliminary renting bullshit. He sighed. This wasn't the job for him, if any job could be. He liked the hours to himself. Being his own boss. Minus the owners, of course, but they were never in town. He'd send them some pictures when the place was set. Then, he'd take a few days off and sit in the air conditioning and just answer the phone. IF he answered it. He laughed, dumping what was left of his breakfast into the trash. Throwing on a pair of jeans and a wife beater, he dug through a few boxes in the storage room for an old pair of work gloves. That and a trowel and he was ready to pretend he had a green thumb.

He dropped the mail on his office desk and went into his living room. Sweaty, tired and done. That low-grade headache was hanging on but at least the plants were in. Bills could wait till tomorrow. That's all there were anyway, and they didn't pay him overtime to work night hours. At least they weren't his bills. Joe shook his head. He'd have to talk to the owners about upping his salary. He had blindly scooped up the job when it came along. Took the first offer they put out. He knew he could handle it and he fucking needed a steady paycheck. Lately, though, it never seemed enough.

He plopped down onto the sofa and thought about what he wanted to do. TV, head over to Rudy's for a drink. It'd been a while since he'd gone out. Maybe there'd be some cute thing to help him forget his troubles for a night. Or create new ones. Damn. All he wanted was some sex, not a morning after wake up and a "when are you going to call me" moment. No fucking entanglements. Just some heart pounding, cock twitching sex. Screw it. He chuckled at the irony. At the very least, he could have a beer and then decide.

Joe opened the refrigerator and had to smile. Six eggs, a half pack of American cheese and twenty beers. There might be a couple of slices of pizza wrapped up in the back. Or Chinese food. Damn, that was bad. If you don't know what's under the foil, it's been in the fridge too long. He grabbed a beer, leaving the mystery food alone. That'd be for when he cleaned. Or if. The fridge door swung shut as he dug through his junk drawer for a bottle opener.

"Should've gotten twist offs," he said. Finding the opener, he popped off the cap and took a long swallow.

Now that was good. Exactly what he needed. Maybe after a few he'd walk to Rudy's. Maybe. He might even go with beer goggles on. Get some nachos, maybe end up with some head in the alley before coming home. That'd be cool. And useful. Don't bring 'em home if you don't want 'em. He was getting used to being single and it wasn't half bad.

Joe turned, the open beer in his hand and two unopened ones tucked under his arm, and saw the spirit board sitting on the kitchen table. "Well, now," he muttered. "Guess I could waste a little time here while the beer catches up. Have a little chat with the resident ghost." He set the bottles beside the board, lit the candles and put his fingers on the planchette.

He paused, trying to think of what to ask.

"Anyone here with me tonight?"

A wait.

"Come on. Black, how about you? Are you here tonight?"

He enjoyed using the board. Even if it was all in his head, power of suggestion and all. He guessed something in his subconscious thought it'd be cool to have a ghost named Black. The slight vibration he noticed the first time he tried the board was more prevalent now. Like an energy, or electricity, running through his fingers; like a car engine trying to turn over. The planchette started to move under his fingertips; first in a circle, then to the alphabet.

"Wait, wait," Joe jumped up and opened his junk drawer. He fished around until he found a pencil and small pad of paper that read Tim Morris for Highway Superintendent and tossed them on the table. As if he'd ever vote. Flexing his fingers, he said, "Now I'm ready."

I am here

"So…what are you doing here?"

Helping you

"Help? What help do I need?"

Life

"And you can help with that?"

Yes

"What can a ghost do to help me? Or, are you telling me you're some sort of angel?" Joe snorted. He'd never believed in angels, or in God, for that matter. This thing must be pulling his leg.

The planchette circled again before landing on the word *Yes.*

"You're fucking pulling my leg. My guardian angel, with the name of Black?" he laughed. "Sounds like a bad horror movie."

Sure

"What am I drinking tonight?"

Beer

"Can you tell my future?"

Easily

"Well…go for it. Give me some lottery numbers of something."

No

"Son of a bitch," Joe said. He took his right hand off the planchette to grab a beer. "All right, how do I know you're really here? Really real? I could be pushing this thing around the board myself. Subconsciously or some shit. Prove it to me."

Of course

"Of course? Okay…" he glanced around. "Blow out the candle."

The candle went out in a puff, as if someone had their mouth right next to it and let just enough air escape their lips to kill the flame. Joe stared. He had never expected it to go out. Some part of his mind was sure he was making up this little game.

"Coincidence. What else can you do?"

You want parlor tricks

"Parlor tricks? What year do you think this is? I want proof. Something that shows me I'm talking to more than my own insanity."

Be careful what you ask for

"Prove to me you're here," Joe said. He shivered. The room seemed a little colder now. He listened for a second and realized the air conditioner wasn't on.

On the desk in the morgue

"Morgue? You mean my office. It hasn't been a morgue in years."

are some letters

"Go on. There are always letters on desks."

Bills

"That's not proof. I know those things. I read the envelopes." He took the last swallow from the bottle and grabbed the next beer on the table. "Just a minute, Black. I have to open this one." Popping the top off, he returned his fingers to the planchette. The vibration continued.

There is money for you

"What? No way!" Joe strode into his office and rifled through the pile of mail on his desk. He opened one that was hand addressed to Forest View. Inside was a check in the amount of $750, made out to Joseph Paine. The memo said "security." What the actual hell? How did they make THAT mistake? Sure, he'd been the one showing people around, but the workers had barely finished. He didn't even think it had been fully advertised yet. He turned the check over in his hands. Would they even miss it? He would be the one taking the rent, making the deposits. The owners didn't want to handle the little details. These people could move in, pay their rent…he'd probably be long gone by the time they wanted to move out and had any thought about their security deposit. And he had been down on his luck lately.

He tucked the check into his shirt pocket and returned to the kitchen. If he started to feel guilty about it he could replace it later on. When his luck was better. Or not. He sat down in front of the board and stretched out his arms, cracking his knuckles.

"Well, Mr. Black," he said. "You were right." He rested his fingertips on the planchette.

You are welcome

"You're not telling me that you *did* this."

Yes

"Well. Thanks?"

You will repay me

"What is this, The Godfather? How do I give anything to a ghost?"

You will
This I require

The planchette circled the board landing once in each of the four corners before coming to a stop. Joe sat, staring at it, then took the check out of his pocket. He wasn't sure exactly what a ghost would want but what the hell. He'd deposit the check in the morning. For now, a little TV was in order.

He slipped a couple more beers under his arm, fumbled with the opener and walked into the living room. Flipping the light switch off with his elbow, he positioned the bottles in a row beside the recliner and settled in. As he leaned backward, the remote fell and hit the floor. Joe sighed, twisted around and grabbed it. The power button was worn dull and he pressed it without looking down, squinting as his eyes adjusted to the brightness.

"TV's better in the dark, eh, Black?" It was cozy in the TV light. Comfortable. Joe channel surfed for a minute before clicking on ESPN. "I hope you like sports," he muttered.

5

As Dom drove, the afternoon sun would've been completely annoying if he hadn't had his sunglasses. It was a shame that he couldn't have coordinated the drive with Amanda since the two of them were hitting Centerville today, but she had left first thing in the morning to get a jump on things. The road signs passed by, one after another, with an unending tree line. He enjoyed the ride. Music turned up, a nice mix of '80's and '90's, air conditioner running. All good. He had brought a voice recorder and hoped that Jay wouldn't mind if he recorded the walkthrough. It was easier than taking notes, re-asking questions to make sure he had it all down. This way, it was there. Ready to be transcribed, listened to, whatever, as many times as necessary. As the miles wore down, he kept an eye out for the Centerville exit.

He pulled into the carport beside 11 Ridley, got out and looked around. His was the only vehicle; Jay must be running a few minutes late. No matter, he'd have a look around and take some photos of the exterior. The lawn was mowed and a "For Sale" sign was stuck into the ground by the road. It definitely wasn't a mover, pretty drab on the outside. The paint, while not peeling, had gotten dingy. Something he would have addressed if he were the agent trying to sell the place. Or maybe not. If your clients were more concerned with the murder of the last owner, they probably would overlook it needing a fresh paint job.

He did a quick walk around the back. There was no lawn

furniture to be seen, no grill, no homey touches outside, with small, dark basement windows. That the house was at the end of a lonely dead end seemed fitting. Something right out of a horror novel, if you asked him. Intriguing. He snapped a few photos of the windows, the yard. A dark gray, almost blue, cat sat on the edge of the tree line, watching him.

"Hey, kitty, kitty," he squatted down and held out his hand. "Come on, pussy cat." It almost looked like the cat was considering it when they both heard the sound of an engine settling and a car door shutting. Dom stood and walked back around the side of the house. A small white Corolla had parked beside his van, and a man in a yellow polo shirt stood next to it.

"Mr. Giordano" the man called out.

"Call me Dom," he walked up, arm outstretched to shake hands with the guy.

"Did you find the place alright?" They shook. Dom was pleased it was firm. Weak ones left him wanting to wipe off his hand on his pants. A pet peeve of his, bordering on phobic. You could tell a lot about a person from their handshake.

"Yeah, not a problem. I was giving it a quick look while I waited."

Jay turned toward the house. "Not an impressive structure, is it?" He sighed, letting his realtor persona drop. "And definitely not a quick turn around on the market." He took out his keys and went up the side steps. They walked into the kitchen together. Jay left the door open to give them a little fresh air, even with the heat. It was stuffy inside, but that was to be expected. Any place not running air conditioning at this point in the summer would be the same.

The kitchen was as dull as the outside of the house. A little dusty, with long countertops, a refrigerator, kitchen table and chairs. Nothing fancy; nothing that stood out as unusual or unique. A kitchen. In a murder house. He didn't know what he had expected when he walked in. He'd done quite a few private investigations, but none with such a tragic history. Now, it would be his job to try to pull something out of that tragedy, some communication with who or whatever had been there. Or debunk it.

"Do you mind if I record our walkthrough? It helps later when I want to go over everything with the team."

Jay waved off the question. "Sure, that's fine."

Dom nodded and took the recorder out of his shirt pocket. He turned it on, watching the red light blink for a few seconds, making sure it was set. "So, Jay. What can you tell me about the history here?"

"Yeah, I suppose we should get to the point of why we're here. I naturally go into 'home showing mode' once I walk into a building." He paused for a moment. "Jack Barnes was the last owner. I think he was here about 12-ish years? He was found, dead, right over here." Jay moved to the middle of the kitchen floor. "It was a blood bath. The guy had the shit beaten out of him. Took a cleaning team to get it all up." He looked at Dom. "Sorry."

"No, no. I need all the information I can get. Any details you can give me are great." Dom took some photos of the kitchen, especially the area where the body had been found. Not to find anything paranormal but to document. He was a stickler for going in prepared, researched and informed.

"It seems that the police found him in his buddy's arms. They also came across a journal that Jack had kept, detailing the abuse the guy had given him and it seemed to completely implicate Parker Davies as the murderer." Jay's voice got a little quieter, a little more tense. "But at the trial, the guy couldn't be shaken in his testimony. He swore he was innocent, not that they don't all swear it when they're faced with life in prison, I guess. But he was adamant that Jack had brought something back from the asylum with him. Something evil that had thrown things, moved furniture, attacked him multiple times before killing him. He said the journal that Jack had kept had been a diary of his investigation information and nothing else. That whatever killed him had changed it somehow."

"The asylum?"

"New Castle. In Fremont. Seems it was the last place that Jack had done a ghost hunt. Davies said that Jack brought back a Ouija board or something and that was where a lot of this trouble had started. He had gone through the evidence that Jack brought back…that there were video and audio recordings, and that they had printed out photos showing some shadow guy or something."

Dom raised an eyebrow. "A Ouija board?" He glanced around.

"It's not here. Was never found."

"Interesting." Dom's inner investigative senses came alive when Jay mentioned a Ouija board. Many investigations hinged on issues with the occult, people dabbling where they should have left well enough alone. All you had to do was google spirit boards and you'd be scrolling for days through "Ouija gone bad" experiences. True or not, the reports were staggering. "Do you know what they did with Jack's equipment?"

"I assume they took what they needed for evidence. It's probably still held by the court system somewhere. There's a storage unit with some of his belongings, waiting for auction. The only family he had was a brother in Missouri, and he said there was nothing here he wanted. If you'd like to go through the unit, I'm sure I can get permission for you to check it out. I really don't know what's there, though."

"Yeah, that'd be great. It would be amazing if we found something related to that last investigation." Damn, he would love to have access to that. It could speak to Barnes' state of mind and give them a peek into what he was truly dealing with, paranormal or not.

"I don't know if you'll find what you're looking for," Jay said. "It may just be some furniture and household stuff."

"Not a problem. I'm willing to take the chance and make an offer if it's something we can use."

"You got it," Jay agreed. He typed a quick message on his phone.

"A reminder to check with the brother when I get back to the office. He really wants to be done with all this." He motioned to the house. "Would you be able to run over like an hour or two before the investigation?"

"Absolutely." Dom was thrilled. If there was even a chance they could find something pertinent, this could be the smoking gun they needed. "So, were you at the trial? Or are you that well read?"

Jay laughed. "I was in the courtroom every day. It may sound morbid, but it was one of the most interesting things to happen in this town in years. A lot of us went."

They stepped through the archway into the living room.

Dom's phone vibrated. He glanced at the number and said, "Excuse me, do you mind? It's my team." Jay shook his head and walked into the bedroom. Dom swiped the answer button. "Yeah."

"Dom."

"Hey, Bri. I'm with Jay. What's up?"

"Ammie wanted me to give you a quick call. There seems to be a connection between Jack and this…New Castle Asylum. It's in Freemont but it's got some link to the murder."

"Yeah, it does. I can tell you about it when I get back."

"Great! Ammie found a passenger who knew this Barnes guy."

"Very nice. Seems like it's all going to pull together. I'll call when I get home."

"Sure, man. Later."

He clicked his phone off. "They're pretty excited for this investigation. I sent over some articles I found on the town, murder and trial, seeing what we could piece together. You've been the most help so far, though."

"Glad I could be. What other questions do you have?"

"Do you know where the activity supposedly took place that Davies talked about?"

Jay thought for a minute. "He mentioned that Jack heard footsteps, and there was something to do with the basement door opening and closing on its own. That one freaked me out the most. We've all heard footsteps that we can't explain, but the door moving on its own…" he shuddered. "I can't tell you if that actually happened or not. It might've been in the mind of a murderer, or…" his voice trailed off. "You know what I think?" Jay paused. "I think they put away an innocent man. I've seen men lie before and he wasn't. He was a man terrified. Not for his life, but of what he had seen. Lived through." He looked from the living room to the kitchen, letting his eyes stop on the basement door, almost believing the knob would turn if he left his gaze there too long. "This house gives me the creeps."

Dom smiled. "Yeah." He took mental note of where he wanted to mount the cameras, the areas he'd want to capture when his team came in. They wandered into the living room, then the bedroom. "Any recent remodeling?"

"Nope. It's all the original structure."

Dom opened the closet doors, eyeing the crawlspace cover. "Anything up in the attic?"

"It's pretty tight up there but I think that's where he heard the footsteps."

"We'll probably stick a camera and recorder up there when we come back. Was there any mention of cold spots, electrical issues?"

"Not that I remember. I know that Davies had said some things had moved. The furniture, a bowl."

"Furniture?" Dom's senses peaked again. If something in the house was strong enough to move furniture it was a damned strong entity. If Davies was telling the truth. "Did they ever do anything to address it? Do you know if they brought in a team or cleansed or blessed the house? Was Jack a religious man?"

Jay shook his head. "You're testing my memory. I don't know much at all about the guy."

"Sorry. Trying to explore every thread I can. The more I have going in, the more focused our investigation will be. Even a small detail might be helpful." Dom looked around, raised his eyebrows. "You mentioned the basement?"

Jay took a deep breath. "Let's go." They walked to the basement door and Jay rested his hand on the knob. It was almost an imperceptible hesitation but there nonetheless. Dom noticed his discomfort but before he could offer to go alone, Jay opened the door and started down the steps. He followed into the darkness.

At the bottom of the wooden steps, Jay reached around for the string to turn on the lightbulb. It came on with that familiar *chink* of metal chain. Dom walked carefully down, looking into the dimly lit corners. A washing machine, dryer, some storage space with a few lawn chairs. It was cool and had that damp cobwebby feel. The small windows cast dusty, dull rays of light. He took a few more pictures.

"There's always too many shadows half-hiding in basements like this. Like something is waiting to jump out. I prefer the newer, brightly lit ones, myself," Jay said. "But, I can't sleep with my feet out of the covers, either. And clowns!" he shivered. "This place brings out all my phobias, I guess. I don't know how you guys do it."

"I hate water," Dom said. "You'll never catch me in the ocean…or a pool." He shook his head. "We all have something, I guess. Any reports of activity down here?"

Jay thought hard. "I really don't remember, other than that door." He pointed toward the kitchen, fighting the urge to get back upstairs into the light. He didn't know if he believed in ghosts, but he didn't want to test any theories of them, either. Horror movies made him want to sleep with the lights on, just in case, and anything related to the paranormal gave him the heebie jeebies. He'd be happy to get the house sold and be rid of it, ghosts or not. Relief swept him when Dom started back up to the kitchen.

"Did he own any pets?" Dom ran his hand along the counter and looked out through the window over the sink. The cat he had seen earlier was sitting in the grass about fifteen feet from the carport, staring at the house. He didn't see a collar. Jay joined him.

"Ah, that Russian blue. Gorgeous animal. Hangs around the house but never gets too close," he stepped back. "I'm not sure about Jack. Maybe that's his cat or maybe he's a stray that Jack fed. He never gets close, but, you'll notice when you come back he's out there somewhere."

Dom turned. "So, when would we be able to come in and investigate?"

"When can you? I'd like to get this done as soon as possible so I can move on with it all."

"We can be back as soon as tomorrow night. Once we've got all the data collected, it does take some time to go through. As soon as we do, we'll meet to show you our findings."

"Great. That sounds great. What time works for you? We can meet here and run over to the storage unit first. It's about ten minutes away and shouldn't take that long to look through. I can meet you here at…5:00 p.m.? Is that too early? I know all the ghost shows have people investigating late at night."

"Unfortunately, ghosts don't run on schedule," Dom chuckled. "5:00 p.m. would be fine. It'll take us a while to get the equipment set up, get the cameras placed. It's nice to get that done early."

"Cool. I really appreciate this."

"No problem. We're here to help."

They continued outside and Jay locked the door to the house. "Really, Dom. Thanks." He placed one hand on Dom's shoulder and shook the other.

Dom smiled. "You're welcome. We'll see you here tomorrow." He glanced at the back yard as he went to his car. The cat was there, sitting on a rock under the trees. Still watching. He adjusted his rearview mirror, bringing the animal into view. It had taken a few steps closer to the house, keeping an eye on the carport. "No worries, kitty. We're leaving," Dom said under his breath. He turned the mirror back into position and placed the key into the ignition.

His mind was spinning, turning around all the information he had gotten. Putting it together, looking for clues, thinking what might be debunked. Fact, the guy had been gruesomely murdered in his kitchen. Fact, his best friend had been arrested, found guilty, sent to prison and was found dead last year. Fact, the guy had been on a ghost hunt at an asylum a few weeks prior to his death. Fact, they may be able to put their hands on something that Barnes had actually come across that would blow the doors off this investigation. He hit the steering wheel. He had to pull himself back to reality. They probably wouldn't find anything useful in that storage unit. Dom rolled it around his mind. They'd need to research New Castle and see what they could dig up there. Maybe he and Amanda could work on that tomorrow. He loved being the Watson to her Sherlock Holmes.

Twenty-seven miles to go. There was a McDonalds off the next exit and he took it rather than listen to his stomach growl for the next half hour. Fast food had never been his favorite, but it filled the need. There were two cars ahead of him, a tired mom with kids in tow, and teens, probably grabbing something quick to eat on their way to the movies or to hang at the mall. He inched along, waiting through their orders of multiple burgers, fries, nuggets and shakes, when all he wanted was a grilled chicken sandwich and an unsweetened tea. Finally, he pulled up to the speaker.

The voice behind the microphone was obviously tired, annoyed and frazzled. He smiled. Orders and changes, you didn't give me this and I ordered that, can I have this instead? It'd make him nuts on a good day. He paid at window one and slowly rolled ahead to the next, where the tired voice handed him his order. "Have a good night," he said, then winked. "Don't let 'em get to you." The girl looked up and grinned. He got back on the highway and ate as he drove.

His mind went back to the investigation tomorrow night. The Barnes house. It was time to push the facts out of the way and see where the hearsay left him. Footsteps, furniture being moved, the basement door opening and closing. He was intrigued but skeptical. He approached every investigation with a healthy dose of skepticism. It was his M.O. to go in with as many facts as possible, then look at the reports of activity and endeavor to explain them away scientifically. That cold spot by Grandpa's chair? Check for drafts. An old window not sealed well. A floor vent long forgotten. That periodic banging sound? Heat pipes rattling. Rodents sneaking in for a late-night snack. A door opening on its own? Loose latch, poorly hung. A change in air pressure when another door in the house is opened…There were tons of possibilities that needed to be explored before labeling anything a haunting. It brought to mind Data playing Sherlock Holmes in a Star Trek Next Generation episode. "Once you eliminate the impossible, whatever remains, no matter how improbable, must be the truth." Sir Arthur Conan Doyle's quote would still be appropriate in the 23rd century. The corners of his lips turned up, just slightly. He was such a nerd.

Ghost hunting was a learning process, too. That's probably what he loved the most, aside from finding proof of a haunting, of course. It was a shame he didn't get paid for all the hours he put in. It was all good, though. He wouldn't change a thing.

He pulled into his parking space. Grabbing his camera off the passenger seat, he picked up the fast food bag and paper cup. A last mouthful of half tea, half melted ice and he was on his way. Dom nodded at his neighbors as he went up the sidewalk to the back door of the building. A few of the moms were watching their kids climb on the monkey bars off to the side by the swings. He loved the long late-summer evenings with fall around the corner. He took the cement steps two at a time, ducking in the doorway under the yellowed light that came on each night at 7:00 p.m.. In another few hours, the moths would be casting eerie silhouettes onto the tiny playground. He stopped to check his mailbox before continuing up the two flights to his hallway.

The corridor looked like a cross between an old time hotel and a college dorm and, if he thought about it, his apartment wasn't much different. 317. Gold numbers painted on a brown metal door. He turned the key, heard the tumbler click into place and went inside. It was a small one bedroom but it was all he needed. A kitchen, a living room…somewhere for his equipment and a place to sleep. He corrected papers at the kitchen table or took care of schoolwork from his laptop. The college was trying to keep up with the times and more and more was required online. He didn't mind. He could be a tech-head when necessary.

Dom dropped his mail onto the kitchen table, envelope by envelope. Bill, bill, bill… yeah, it was that time of the month again. He smirked. He set down his camera, took his phone out of his pocket and dialed Brian. Amanda picked up.

"Jerk's phone, Amanda here."

Dom laughed. "Hey, kiddo. I'm home."

"Bri, get your ass over here. Dom's on the phone," she yelled. "What's up? What'd you find out? When do we go in?"

"How's tomorrow night sound? 5 p.m."

"Are you kidding me?"

He could hear Brian in the background. "What? What's he saying? Ammie, gimmie my damn phone." Dom rolled his eyes. He didn't know how they hadn't killed each other yet. Amanda was yelling.

"Damn it, Bri! Give it back."

"Hey, Dom. It's me," Brian said.

"Hey."

"So, we're in? When?"

"Tomorrow night. 5 p.m."

"What'd you find out?"

"Put me on speaker. I'm not doing this double time," He waited until he heard the familiar change over and almost echo-like tone of the speaker. "Hey, guys."

A two-person chorus of "Hey, Dom" came back at him. It was

funny how they could be such kids, but as soon as they hit an investigation, they were absolute professionals and truly good at what they did.

It was hard to contain his excitement. "There's a storage unit with Barnes' belongings and I may have access."

"What?!" again, the chorus. "Are you kidding?"

"Dead serious. Fingers crossed we find something."

"Equipment? Do you think his equipment is in there?" Brian asked. To be able to go through Barne's ghost hunting equipment would be so cool. As tech guy, he was always keeping an eye out for the newest gadget.

"I don't know. That might have been confiscated by the court for the trial. I'm sure his computer is history. But we'll be able to see things from the house the way it was at the time of the murder. At the very least get a feel for it all. Best case scenario we find something that can help us figure out what really happened there."

"So cool! Can I go with you instead of with Ammie? Ow! Damn, Sis," Brian complained.

"We're going to have to put in some research time tomorrow on New Castle Asylum," Dom began.

"In Fremont," Amanda continued for him. "Yeah, we saw it mentioned as having a part in the trial."

"It sure did. Seems it was the last place that Barnes investigated before he was killed."

"Interesting," Brian said. "So, the thought is he went there and brought something nasty back with him?"

"Yeah. Also, there was some talk of a Ouija board but none was ever found in the house. I'm not sure if that was rumor or not."

"It's a shame Davies is dead. Would've been nice to maybe get in and talk to him directly," Brian said.

"Would've made things easier, for sure," Dom said. "But I think we've got a good amount to go on for tomorrow night. I've gone through the entire house minus the attic crawlspace. I think we'll need a camera up there. Supposedly there were footsteps heard, furniture moved, a door opening and closing. We'll have to cover the basement and especially the kitchen area, where they found the body."

Amanda spoke up. "This is pretty serious. I don't think we've had anything with such a violent history before."

"Exactly," Dom agreed. "What did you turn up?"

"A couple of things… they may or may not be relevant. Barnes' boss said he was never absent but was out sick the week before he died. The flu or something."

"If he was tangled up with something negative, it could've done that," Brian suggested.

"It's possible," Amanda said. "Also, I met a little old woman who was a regular on Barnes' route. Her name was…" she looked through her notes. "Mabel Trumbel. Sweet thing. Sensitive, too. She recognized it in me."

"Oh?" Dom was intrigued. Amanda rarely talked about her psychic side.

"Yeah. She said that Barnes wasn't crazy. She felt something dark around him and said she had even cautioned him to be careful."

"This just keeps getting better," Dom said. "Makes me really want to know the history of the asylum he visited."

"Makes me want to go there," Brian said. "Maybe we'll need a follow up investigation at New Castle."

"It's not there anymore, Bri. They tore it down and put in an apartment building or something."

"Maybe we can investigate the apartment building. If there's something nasty there, it's not going to go away just because the landscape changed. A lot of times remodeling can escalate activity."

Amanda nodded and Dom said, "Let's see what we're dealing with at the house and then decide. We can check its history tomorrow."

"I want to get to Centerville early and see if I can find Barnes' girlfriend. He was dating someone who worked at one of the restaurants. It couldn't hurt to stop by there and see if she's around."

"Do you know her name?" Dom asked.

"Nope, but I don't think it'll be a problem. Someone must remember her, and who knows? She might still be there."

"Cool. So, I'll swing by around 3:00 p.m. to get Brian and load the equipment into the van and we'll take two vehicles. Meet us at the Barnes house by 7:00 p.m."

"Sounds great! Hopefully we'll both come in with a lot to work with," Amanda said. Then, the chorus, "Night, Dom!"

He rolled his eyes. "Night, guys." Dom clicked off the call. He sighed and glanced around the apartment. It was still early. He opened his laptop and typed in "New Castle Asylum."

6

The Ouija board and planchette were arranged on the kitchen table when he walked into his apartment. He hadn't left them there. He knew he hadn't left them there. He always put them back on the shelf after chatting with the resident ghost. Joe was intrigued but a little uneasy. A ghost can't move things, can it? How does some disembodied voice MOVE things? He eyed the board for a minute and walked into the bedroom.

"If you're that eager to have a talk, you're going to have to wait till after I have a bath," he called out. "And maybe a beer or two." Or five, he thought. He had taken this job thinking it would be cushy. Get the workers in, get everything set, rent the place out and let it run itself. Hah. Disorganized crews, materials not in on time, one thing put off another. A royal pain in the ass. At least it kept fucking food on the table while the bank figured out what it was going to do about the house he left. Whatever. He threw his clothes into a pile on the bathroom floor and turned on the faucet.

The sound of water flowing got to him, as it always did, and he lifted the toilet seat to pee. Relief flooded him as he stood there, eyes shut, letting go of the stresses of the day. He flicked his penis, not caring that the last few drips hit the back of the seat and turned to get into the tub. "What the ever-loving fuck!" The water was brown. Not some drab yellow or off beige, but dirt brown. He quickly turned off the water and hit the lever to open the drain as the smell hit him. "Damn it!" Gagging, he strode naked through his kitchen, living room and out into his office, grabbing the phone on his desk. Thumbing through his papers, he found the number for Murray Water Specialists, the guys who had renovated the plumbing.

It rang. Five, six… come on! On the seventh ring, they answered. He hit the ground running. "Yeah, this is Joe Paine over at Forest View. We've got one hell of a problem over here."

A woman's voice greeted him. "Hello, Mr. Paine, what's the problem?"

"The water's running brown."

"Oh, that's not good. Didn't the men finish things there about a week ago?"

"Yeah, they did, and no, it's not good. I ran a tub and the water is brown. Shit brown. And I mean that. It smells like it's tapped into the septic or something."

"Well, I can get a message to Mr. Murray and have him give you a call back."

"Yeah, thanks. Tell him I need this fixed ASAP. I can't have people coming to see the place without running water. And I can't live here without it in the meantime."

"I'll have him get back to you as soon as he can, Mr. Paine."

Joe hung up the phone and realized he was standing naked at his desk. He laughed. Couldn't do that once the tenants moved in. He walked back into his apartment. Pulling on a pair of boxers, he went to the fridge. Not much there called out to him, but he guessed he'd microwave some leftover Chinese food. A little reheated chicken chow mein and a couple of beers should hit the spot while he waited for the plumber. His eyes fell onto the board as the seconds counted down on the microwave. He sighed. "Well, Mr. Black, I guess it's you and me tonight." The hairs on the back of his neck prickled. Almost. Like that breeze that you don't quite feel, you just sense. It seemed a little cooler, too. Well, it was always a little cooler down in his space. Probably all in his mind. Being in the basement conjured up the idea of cool summer nights, but the fact that his apartment used to be part of the morgue of an abandoned asylum, well… that had its own conjurings. If he was one of those jerks who got bothered by stuff like that. Not him. He was a horror movie addict. Give him a good old blood and guts B movie, decapitations and killer clowns, and he was happy as a pig in shit. Yeah, it didn't matter to him what had happened back in the old asylum days. People died all the time. Big deal. It's not like they were going to get up and walk again. He didn't buy into the zombie apocalypse shit.

The microwave dinged and broke his train of thought. He stirred the chow mein, burning his fingers on the edge of the bowl. It dropped to the table with a bang, next to the board. "Chow mein, Mr. Black?" He paused, wondering if his ghost buddy hung around when he wasn't there. Stupid thought, duh, who else put out the Ouija board? He'd been having some fun with it all, trying to see if Black would talk with him. Crazy ass parlor game. He never thought it'd really work. He cracked open a beer and sat down.

He absently took a mouthful of his dinner when he heard a SLAM. Joe jumped, hitting the bowl and spilling chow mein across his bare leg. "What the hell?" He swiped at his thigh then ran back out through the living room and into the office. It sounded like a metal door swinging shut. Like a big, old metal door hitting hard against the jam. He stopped. There was nothing like that here. All the doors were new and the floors were that indoor outdoor carpet that had a way of muting every sound. What the living hell could it have been?

He left his office and slowly walked down the hallway into the storage area. Nothing. Nothing that could even remotely sound like that. He wracked his brain for anything on the upper two floors that might have mimicked the noise. Coming up empty, he went back to his apartment. He swore it sounded like an old metal door. No matter. He supposed he could be hearing things, remembering it wrong. Something like that. He tried to let it go and popped open the next beer.

He was eager to see what Black would say tonight. Black. He smirked. Kind of an ominous, cliché type name. But, if that's what he wanted to call himself, fine. Made it all the more interesting. Joe wiped his hands on his boxers, took a lighter off the counter and lit the little candle he kept out for his Ouija board sessions. Sessions. Damn, had he done it enough that it was now a thing? He guessed so. He rested his fingers on the planchette.

"Well, Mr. Black, are you here with me tonight?" He paused, waiting for the familiar vibration to begin under his fingertips. It would start as a barely perceptible hum beneath his fingers. Tonight, however, when the planchette began to circle across the board, he felt a coolness, like a cold hand, over his. Like someone leaning over him, arm along his, hand resting over his own, controlling the planchette. If he concentrated, he could sense, almost *feel*, breath beside his ear. He shoved the planchette across the table, turning quickly to see who was behind him. Of course there was no one. He tried to shake off the feeling, but it had given him the creeps. "Fuck you," he muttered. Glancing around, the room still didn't feel right. Like he was being watched. "Asshole ghost."

He grabbed a pack of cigarettes off the counter and shook one out. The lighter was still beside the candle on the table. He gave the spark wheel a quick roll and stared at the flame. Orange and flickering yellows trying to coalesce into…something. He lit the cigarette, drawing in a breath and snapped the lighter shut. He didn't like fire. A friend of his had told him once that you could see faces in flames. And right now, he wasn't in the mood.

He exhaled and let the smoke rise above the board. "Was that you, Black? You can keep your damn hands to yourself." Knocking some of his ashes into melted wax of the candle, he continued. "Let's keep the convo to the board, got it?" A cool breeze blew across him making the candle flicker wildly and another door slammed.

"Shit," he remembered the mess in the tub. "Damn it!" He strode into the bathroom, trying to decide what cleanser he'd have to use to get the tub halfway sanitary again. He'd need some rubber gloves. Yellow ones like in the Lysol and Mr. Clean commercials. It'd almost be funny if he didn't have to scrub a shit filled bathtub. He flipped on the light. "What the goddamned fuck?" The tub was full. Of water. Clean, clear water. There was no sign of anything, brown or otherwise, ever having been in there. Christ, it was cleaner than before he had turned on the tap. Was he losing his mind? Joe sat on the toilet and leaned back. He trailed his fingers in the water, letting it drip back into the tub. Every drop as crystal clear as the last. No. He knew what he had seen. Knew what he had *smelled.* Maybe he was going crazy. Maybe he needed to get to a doctor. Anxiety formed a knot in his stomach at the thought. He took a long drag on his cigarette and let the smoke out of his lungs slowly.

His stomach growled. The chow mein was probably cold by now. Well, that's what microwaves were for, right? The bachelor life. As he stood, there was a loud crash in the kitchen. He sprinted. The bowl was in the middle of the floor, broken; his dinner mixed among the shards. "Must've left it on the edge. Figures," he muttered. But he hadn't. It had sat fully on the table where he'd dropped it. While he cleaned up the mess, the thought nagged at the back of his mind. He pushed it away. He couldn't be losing his mind and he wouldn't believe it was anything else.

The slivers of glass chinked as they slid into the garbage. He tossed the dustpan into the sink with the dirty dishes and grabbed some paper towels to wipe down the floor. What was he going to eat tonight? To hell with it. Another beer and a half-eaten bag of potato chips would do it. He was done with the day. Weary. Worn out. He sat at the table and fixed his eyes on the board, wondering if he was losing his mind.

7

Dom woke and tossed off the red, yellow and green patchwork afghan that covered him. It was the one splash of color in an otherwise Zen, but borderline drab, living room. He kept it on the back of the couch for nights like this, thanks to his sister. She had given it to him one Christmas and when he got tired, especially after working on the computer late at night, he tended to curl up right where he was…on the sofa, near his laptop. Sleep was never an issue. Once he got tired, he could sleep anywhere. If he was cozy, especially late at night, he'd doze off, on the couch, on a friend's sofa, it didn't matter. Missed a lot of movies that way. He liked his bed but wasn't tied to it. He laughed. Nope, the handcuffs were for date night.

He stretched, and walked into the kitchen. Coffee time. He turned on the faucet and grabbed the pot. His only vice. He fumbled in the package for a filter and stuffed one into the Mr. Coffee basket. He stared at the wall while he waited for the water to fill to the ten-cup line. A window would be nice, with a back yard. A hammock. He didn't mind the bachelor life, in fact he thrived on it, but there was something to be said for having a lawn to mow with maybe some rows of veggies planted. Instead, he faced rows of doors when he stepped through his own. Dom shoved the pot into position over the heating element. Ten cups. Yeah, that might do. He flipped the unit on. A big cup of coffee in the morning, or, hell, anytime, put him into the right frame of mind. Caffeinated.

He sat back down on his couch and saw that he had left his

laptop on. It had gone into sleep mode at some point and he was glad that he left it plugged in. Like his phone. If something could be charged, it should be, in his opinion. He hated letting his electronics run down, just as he never let his gas tank get below a half. Such a freaking boy scout, he thought. Always prepared.

His computer came back to life as he listened to the coffee bubbling in the kitchen. The room filled with the aroma of the living as he reached over to his printer to grab the pages he sent there last night. He had gotten a pretty good picture in his mind of what New Castle had been about. Originally built in 1893, it had housed the "mentally feeble." It was much smaller than most institutions at the time, presumably for richer families who could afford to "shuffle off" their loved ones, who believed they were doing "everything they could," yet not have to deal with them personally. He shuddered at that mentality. As with most places of its kind, it had become overcrowded, under staffed, and the people residing there were not well cared for. Now THAT was an understatement. Dom had seen documentaries on similar sites and it was tragic bordering on terrifying at times.

New Castle itself was closed down in 1987 and remaining patients were moved to other facilities more geared to their specific care. Over the years it had fallen into disrepair, with vandals, vagrants and curiosity seekers sneaking onto the grounds off and on, causing trouble. He'd found a few articles mentioning the vandalism, particularly on the second floor, and hints of darker things. Possibly satanic. Nothing was said outright, but there were allusions in the articles, mentions of graffiti, pentagrams and candles. It was as if the reporter was fearful of the subject and had no idea what it all meant.

There were a few mentions of New Castle in the articles about the trial but mainly in passing as something Davies had referenced. He hoped there would be something more in that storage unit. He got his coffee and stepped out into the little alcove the complex called a balcony. It was already getting warm, but the humidity was low. A perfect end of summer day. He tossed around the idea of going for a run. He definitely had that anxious, excited nervousness flowing through his veins and a run would calm him, even temporarily. Investigations always got him ramped up.

He put his empty cup into the sink and headed for the bedroom. Shorts, a tank top and a quick hunt for his running shoes and he was out the door. He slow jogged around the perimeter of the parking lot and took a path through the trees at the far end. It had been there since long before he had moved in and was well worn. He enjoyed its freshness, the wildflowers, and the shade of the overhanging trees. It was an uneven dirt path and you had to be especially watchful around some turns not to twist an ankle on the occasional root. Here and there he'd pass a clearing. The kids from the complex liked to build forts among the bushes, and probably the older ones used them to smoke weed without being seen.

He continued on, working up a good sweat and letting his mind sort out the night's investigation. The cameras would go in the kitchen, basement, crawlspace, and one facing into the kitchen, focused on the basement door. He hadn't decided yet where they'd set up their base camp to monitor the cameras and keep track of the equipment. As he thought about the house, he came out of the woods and into the east end of the parking lot. It was a good thirty-minute loop and he kept his pace, heading back for a second go round.

Dom kept an eye for the tree roots and watched the squirrels sprinting through the trees as he moved along the trail. Once in a while he'd cross paths with a deer, and he'd heard someone saw a black bear a few years ago, but those were rare. He checked his watch and took his pulse, all good. The path was dry and he was kicking up little clouds of dirt as he ran. It reminded him of dust and that led to thinking about what could be packed away in Barnes' storage unit. He couldn't wait to get his hands on it.

He looped back through the parking lot and took the steps two by two. Inside his apartment, he started the shower and let it run while he pulled out his clothes. Fresh jeans and a black shirt with the Out of the Dark logo. He'd wear a pair of black boots, too. Professional casual. He laid the clothes out on the bed. The bathroom was steamy and he stood under the water enjoying the feel of it flowing over him. He lathered slowly, taking in the scent of the soap and the feel of it sliding over his skin, then dropped it into the soap dish. While the rushing water rinsed him off, he visualized any negativity around him being washed off as well. He saw it in his mind, pouring off his skin and circling the drain, finally disappearing. It was something that Amanda had taught him. She was big on grounding and centering. Protections. He believed in her sensitivities and even though it had taken him a while to actually put a few things into practice, they did seem to help. It left him feeling calmer. Less stressed. He turned the water off and reached for a towel.

Dom toweled off his hair and stood in front of the small bathroom mirror. He didn't quite have a six-pack, but he was pretty happy with what he did have. Comfortable in his own skin. At one with the universe. He smiled. Hanging the towel over the shower rod, he went back into the bedroom to get dressed.

He looked around. He needed to download the voice recording with Jay into his computer. He found the cord for his recorder and plugged it into the laptop. Aside from that and his charger, he didn't have much else to throw into the van. Huh. Somehow, all of his equipment had migrated to Brian's. He guessed it didn't matter; Brian was their tech guy. But, it WAS his. He shook his head. Breakfast was calling.

He dropped a couple of pieces of bread into the toaster and turned on the larger burner on the stove. The frying pan was in the dish drainer. A couple of fried eggs on toast with a slice of cheese would be heaven. That and another cup of coffee. He set it all cooking and checked his laptop. It didn't take long for the recording to load and he stood watching the bar as it crossed the screen. He saved it to a file he named "Barnes," and disconnected the recorder. After checking the file and hitting play to verify it worked, he erased what was on the voice recorder. He packed up the few pieces of equipment in his apartment, throwing in a few extra batteries for good measure, and went back into the kitchen in time to slide the eggs out of the pan and onto the toast. He poured the coffee and took both out onto his balcony. It was so pleasant to sit and eat in the quiet. The apartment kids were out playing; the birds were chirping. Up on the third floor, his balcony was among some of the tree tops. Sometimes chipmunks would run by and he'd even had a flying squirrel the winter before. He'd leave out peanuts and it'd come, grab one and leap back to the trees nearby. It was quite amusing to watch. He smiled as he sipped his coffee.

Dom sighed. It was a nice pause to his day, and he tried to get outside on the balcony each morning, but it was time to get moving. Amanda had impressed upon him how important it was to take that calm moment each day. A time where you had a few minutes of peace to clear your mind, rest your consciousness. Connect to the sights and sounds of nature. Now, it was a habit for him. He'd even stood outside in a severe thunderstorm, listening to the rain pound the ground below and watching the ferocity of it all. He slid the glass door open and went back inside, locking it and pulling the drapery shut. The afternoon sun would be hitting that side of the building and his apartment would be an oven later if he left it open. He slung the laptop case over his shoulder and left.

Brian was ready and waiting.

"All charged? Batteries swapped?" Dom asked. He saw that Brian had two cases packed and a bag over his shoulder.

Brian nodded, his mouth full. He finished his chocolate chip cookie and went into the kitchen to swallow some soda. He came out with a cooler.

"Snacks," he said. "I wasn't sure when we'd be able to eat."

Dom laughed. "You're such a boy scout."

"Always."

"Did you really have cookies and soda for breakfast?"

Brian shrugged. "Um, yeah?"

Dom shook his head. "Please tell me Ammie packed the cooler and not you."

Brian cracked a grin. "She might have."

Dom smiled. Brian followed him down to the van and loaded the cases into the back, but deposited the cooler on at his feet. He liked having everything within reach. Especially snacks on a car ride.

"What'd she pack?"

"Some six-inch subs, cookies, soda."

Dom raised an eyebrow as he pulled into traffic.

 Brian sighed. "…and a baggie of veggies to go with your sub and some bottles of water for your healthy ass. You'll have to get your coffee fix on the road."

They laughed. Amanda was always thinking of everyone and he knew this time would be no exception. She planned every detail of their investigations, like he did, and hit the research just as hard. If he had a suggestion, she was two moves ahead waiting for him to jump on board.

They hit the road a little earlier than originally planned. Dom was excited to get to Centerville. Even taking the time to center himself, the excitement was creeping into him. The thought that there might be a piece of Barnes' evidence in that locker, a clue to what might have been going on, was driving him. They entered the highway about the time that Amanda pulled into the parking lot at A Touch of Home.

8

Another day, another fucking dollar. Or at least 50 cents. Joe sat at his desk, shoving stacks of papers around. The bill from Murray's was in. $175 for showing up to tell him there was nothing wrong with the plumbing. At least it would come out of the owners' pocket and not his. Still, it pissed him off. So did all the paperwork that was piling up. He was never meant for a desk job. He needed to be out with the guys, working with his hands. This desk shit was for accountants and skinny little weasels. He threw down his pen and leaned back in his office chair, almost falling over. The springs gave a little bounce and he ran his hands through his hair, balancing himself with a foot hooked under his desk drawer. He needed a break. This place was sucking the life out of him. Living in the basement sucked, too. It was nice enough, but he felt like he was climbing out of a hole every morning…and into another section of the hole to work. Fucking ex-morgue office. Damn.

Maybe a walk would help. Get some fresh air into his lungs, a little exercise. Leave some of the paperwork behind for an hour or two. There was always tomorrow for pencil pushing and phone calls. Joe went up the side stairway, tripped on the top stair and took a three-step lunge into the lobby to keep himself from landing face first on the floor. It was going to be one of those days.

He shoved the main door open and stepped out into the sunshine. It was incredibly bright and he shielded his eyes with his hand. Of course his sunglasses were back in the basement. Where else would they be? He couldn't win; he couldn't even catch a break. Things hadn't gone right for him in any way, shape or form in months. Something had to give and soon or he was going to lose his mind. He looked around. It was about 85 degrees in the shade and humid as hell. What had he been thinking? A walk? Please. All he needed was heat stroke on top of everything else. He turned on his heel and went back inside the air-conditioned lobby, sighed and headed for the West Staircase. His staircase. He should put up a sign, "This way to the dungeon" or "Welcome to my tomb."

He walked down the steps, dragging his feet like a five-year-old told to stand in the corner, and noticed how dimly lit it was; the entire hallway, from his office to the storage room. He couldn't find any bulbs out, but it was definitely darker and he couldn't put his finger on it. Couldn't find the source. Maybe something was screwy with the wiring. Maybe it was his being out in the sun. That had to be it. His eyes hadn't adjusted yet. He shrugged it off and went back to his desk. The phone was already ringing.

He spent the afternoon setting up interviews and background checks for prospective renters and trying to wade through the growing paperwork that needed his attention. And then, the most god awful of it all. Filing. Bills…under B? Under the name of the company? Tenants… under T? Their names in some other section? Contracts… whatever the hell. Another ten minutes and he was going to throw it all in the trash and desk job be damned. He'd had it. He reached into the cup he kept on the edge of his desk for a paperclip, his fingertips coming up against something hard and round. He fished out a gold ring. Odd. He hadn't noticed that before. Maybe one of the workers had lost it and someone dropped it off. But no one had been there recently, and he was sure no one was ever there when he wasn't. Holding it under his lamp, he made out the initials "JPB." No one he knew. Dropping it into his pencil drawer, he made a mental note to forget about it. He locked his office and went through the connecting door to his apartment. Done. If he didn't already drink, this job would drive him to it.

Joe walked into the kitchen and grabbed his pack of cigarettes off the table. He lit one and exhaled. Now that was good. Finally, something he could do right. He sighed. Maybe he could get the owners to buy him a secretary. Hire. Hire him a secretary. A cute little thing who would wear tight skirts and bend way, way down when she filed. Yeah. Like that'd ever happen. If it did, he'd probably get hit with a sexual harassment lawsuit. That was more his type of luck. He pulled his cell phone out of his shirt pocket and dialed one of his painter buddies.

"Yo, Paul," he said when the guy picked up.

"Hey, what's up?"

"I am done with this shitter of a day. Wanna get a couple of beers, maybe play some pool tonight?"

"Hell, yeah. The bar in an hour?"

"Yeah. See you there."

Rudy's was buzzing for a Tuesday night, but, then again, it was always busy. There was something about a place where you could get a beer and hang with friends, or sit at the bar and chill with no one bothering you. Where everyone knows your name, as the song said. There was a hustle and bustle to this place, usually centered around the pool tables but it was light and friendly enough during the week to bring in a family crowd. Paul's truck was in the parking lot and hoped the guy had secured them a table. Inside, Joe saw him immediately and Paul motioned they had the next game.

As he walked by the bar, Joe ordered a beer from a drop dead gorgeous waitress and pointed to where he'd be. She nodded, with a flirty grin that had him locking eyes with her for a second or two longer than he would have otherwise. Sliding up beside Paul, he nodded at the waitress getting his drink.

Paul shook his head. "You don't want to get in with her. She's got a huge boyfriend. Not a friendly one, either."

"Figures." He took his beer when she came by and grabbed a handful of pretzels from the bowl near them. She went to the next table to take some orders and he looked away.

"Bad day, huh?" Paul asked. He started setting up their balls and handed Joe a stick.

"Bad life, it seems."

Paul laughed. "I hear that. Got halfway through a job today and the woman came in saying she 'never authorized that particular shade of blue.'" He made his voice high and shrill imitating her.

Joe smiled. "Sucks all around. Guess it's not just me."

They shot a few balls in silence, not keeping any kind of score. The beers went down easily and it was good to be out of Forest View for a while. Like a weight had been lifted off his back.

"So how do you like working in a converted asylum?"

"What? Oh. Yeah, it's not bad, if you like spending your days in a morgue."

"The morgue? You live in the morgue?"

Joe nodded. "Converted."

Paul laughed. "No thanks. Nope. Not for me."

"You're shitting me."

"Oh, hell no. Especially not with the history that place has. Weird stuff was supposed to have gone on there. Satan worshipping shit. You wouldn't catch me dead in the morgue."

"Nice," Joe laughed.

Paul smiled. "You know what I mean."

"So, no…ghost stuff for you?"

"What do you mean? Wait. Don't tell me you've got some freaky shit happening there."

Joe smiled.

"Fucking tell me, man."

"Ever use a Ouija board?"

"Are you kidding me?"

"Did you?" Joe asked.

"No."

"Well, I've got one. From the original site, before they started construction."

"Have you used it? That shit can bite you in the ass. I've watched Ghost Adventures," Paul said between handfuls of peanuts.

"I've used it. It's fine."

Paul stared at him.

"Really. I've even got my own…"

"What?"

"Ghost."

"Get the fuck out." Paul turned his attention back to the pool table, then couldn't resist. "You don't."

"I do. Calls himself Black."

"No way."

Joe smiled. "Yeah. Pretty damn cool."

"Cool, but not cool. You've got to knock that shit off, man. Burn that thing."

"What the fuck for?"

"I've heard you can open up doorways. Portals or some shit. Things can come through. Scary shit. Man, you need to get rid of it."

"You're a superstitious fuck."

"Maybe I am. But those things are creepy. I'm telling you."

"Why don't you come and try it? I'll introduce you to my ghost."

"To something that calls itself BLACK? Nope. Not me."

Joe smiled. "Really, man. It's cool."

"Yeah, yeah. Be smart. Or I'll be reading about you in the papers. Local man involved in bizarre murder suicide or some demon shit."

They both laughed. "You should come check it out, Paul."

"Yeah, I don't think so. I'm not going down that rabbit hole."

"Chicken shit."

"Better chicken shit than demon bait."

They played for another hour, calling it quits when Paul said he needed to be going, with work the next day. Yeah, work. Joe was beginning to despise that word, but he hung up his cue. He stepped through the front door of Rudy's and held it open for his friend.

"Good seeing you, man," Paul said.

"Yeah, you, too. I'll say hi to Black for you."

"Hah! You do that. And tell him to keep the fuck away from me while you're at it." The two laughed, walking through the parking lot. Joe shook his head. Maybe he'd do just that. It was still early. Perhaps he'd go have a chat with Black.

Joe sat in front of the kitchen table, lighter in his hand, staring at the candle flame. It creeped him out, but tonight it was hard to look away. There was a figure in the fire, dancing and jumping. Mesmerizing, even knowing in his heart it had to be his imagination. It seemed so strange. A weird manifestation of some horror show he watched once. He broke his gaze from the flame and dropped the lighter onto the table beside the spirit board. Placing his hands above the planchette he waited, no longer looking for that hum he had grown used to. Now, before his fingers even touched it, he felt a kind of surge. An energy through his fingertips. Like someone had entered the room through the board, if that made any sense. To him, it was as if Black was with him… a physical, yet invisible, presence. Odd, but how else would a ghost be? There but not there. Maybe he was just more aware now.

He let the energy settle around him. Not that he could have stopped it. It was only polite, though. Invite someone into your home and let them sit down before hitting them with questions.

"Evening, Black."

Salutations

"Well, that's a little formal, isn't it?" Joe asked. He paused for a second, hands hovering over the planchette. "Do I need to use this thing with you? Do you need my energy over the board to work it?"

Hardly

"Well, then," he sat back in his chair and dropped his hands into his lap. "Show me." There was a slight pause and the planchette circled the board once on its own. "Damn," Joe said. "That's so fucking cool." It came to a stop at the center of the board. "So cool."

He paused, wanting to ask all kinds of questions, but his mind was blank with the opportunity at his fingertips. What do you ask when you can ask anything? His mind spun like a tire on gravel.

"So, Black. Where do you come from?" He could almost feel Black roll his eyes. If he had eyes. Where do ghosts come from? Death? Jersey? He smirked. "Spent a week there one afternoon," he said under his breath. The planchette began to slide and he scrambled for his pencil.

Everywhere

"Doesn't answer my question. You can't come from everywhere."

Everywhere
Nowhere

"Do you enjoy talking in riddles?" Nothing. "Come on. How did you get here? Were you passing by and jumped through the board? How's it all work, anyway?"

Come

Was it in his mind's eye or was it happening? His peripheral vision caught a shadow moving through the kitchen and into the living room. He heard, or thought he heard, a gravelly voice whisper.

Come

The non-descript form beckoned to him. He stood, shoving his chair backward with his legs, and followed. It felt like a dream, yet real. They moved, effortlessly, to the main floor, and up the east staircase to the second floor. But it didn't look the way he remembered it. It was older, with paint peeling and bits of plaster on the floor. He walked along the hallway, looking at graffiti on the walls, following this shift of darkness. It didn't make sense, and yet, somewhere in his brain, fit perfectly. He hesitated when three forms took shape ahead of him, at the far end of the hall.

They stood beside the old elevator doors and were drawing a circle on the floor. Black candles were burning and one of the figures held a book. Chanting. Joe couldn't make it out. They had a Ouija board set in the middle of a pentagram that was now scratched into the floor. A ritual. It made him uncomfortable. They also had what looked like an altar of some sort, with a small animal on it. Blood was dripping down the side, and he knew, knew, *knew* there was no mistaking an animal sacrifice. "What IS this?" A rushing wind surrounded him and the figures, and he could feel the utter wrongness growing around them. The air pressure changed. Heavier. He tried to turn but couldn't. Couldn't leave. Couldn't move. His eyes were riveted on the scene Black had brought him to. A shadow formed, grew and coalesced around the figures. He broke out in a sweat, his adrenalin kicking in. His breathing was faster now. He didn't want to see whatever it was they were bringing in. His only thought was to run.

The scene shifted, thank God. The figures were gone; the chanting over. Relief swept through him even though the dark energy remained. He was still near the end of the second-floor hallway; it was still old, broken and abandoned. Still with a pentagram on the floor. But now there was a man in the space with them. Joe recognized him. It was that ghost hunter he had met a while back.

Shook his hand in a Dunkin Donuts once, before….

Before what, Joe?

A voice like broken glass cut through the forefront of his mind.

…before… he was murdered. A cold knot tried to form in his stomach. But that was by his friend. His friend killed him.

Was it?

Again, the voice that made him cringe.

He watched Barnes sit down, a Ouija board in front of him. The Ouija board. It was dark, but he could make it out. He could see it. Recognize it. His. It was his board. His stomach knotted and his mouth went dry. From nowhere, *nowhere*, a shadow crashed into the man, sending his equipment scattering and slamming him into the wall. Whatever it was held him there a few moments before letting him drop to the floor. Joe watched the Barnes' attack as his own fears mounted. And the scene changed again. The energy was stronger now. Barnes was gone. Darkness pressed up against Joe and around him, pushing him against the wall. The pressure made blood pound in his ears and he couldn't catch his breath. He felt himself on the verge of losing consciousness and heard one word whispered into his right ear.

Black

Whatever had been holding him let go and he fell into his chair at the kitchen table. He gripped the sides of the seat and panted, nearly hyperventilating, trying to bring himself back to reality. Trying to get air back into his lungs and not pass out. Could it have been a dream? A hallucination? Was he losing his fucking mind?

Black Black Black Black

It was in his thoughts, yet a part of them. In his head, but loud enough to be in front of him.

"You're not a ghost, are you?"

No

The planchette was motionless. Joe closed his eyes. His hands shook.

I can speak to your thoughts

"No. Go away. I don't want this. I'm done."

The laughter began, swirling through his mind and growing louder. Not a friendly laugh, but a depraved and damnable sound that left him weak. Small. The butt of some malignant joke made by something so much larger than himself.

I will decide when we are done, Joe

And when it used his name, it cut through to his soul. He was stained.

9

It was a homey looking place, with mainly SUV's and family-type cars parked out front. A wood sign hung over the main window of the restaurant, with *"A Touch of Home"* painted in flowing script. Friendly looking. The lot wasn't full, but she arrived in that "after lunch, pre-dinner" lull. Amanda took a deep breath and walked in. She had a game plan in mind and was hungry as well. Fingers crossed this would provide a little more information than they already had.

The hostess met her at the "Please Wait to be Seated" sign and she asked for a booth on the far side next to a window.

"Sure, sweetie," the woman said. She was smartly dressed, her shoulder length ponytail gently swinging as they walked. "Your waitress will be over in a few minutes."

"Thank you." She slid her bag onto the bench beside her and took off her sunglasses before going through the lunch menu, looking for something light and tasty. She settled on a chicken salad sandwich and coffee by the time the waitress showed up with a pitcher of water.

"Afternoon!" the waitress greeted her. "What can I get for you today?"

"Is the chicken salad fresh?"

"Oh, yes. Made this morning and quite delicious."

"Great. That and coffee, please."

"You've got it. I'll be right back with your coffee," the waitress smiled. Amanda read her name tag.

"Thanks, Cindy."

"You're quite welcome," she walked off and Amanda stared out the window. Cindy brought the coffee quickly. She turned over the coffee cup and poured. Amanda ripped open a couple of sugar packets and then grabbed the half and half. She stirred slowly, watching the cars go by on the main road. A few minutes later, Cindy placed her sandwich plate in front of her.

"Thank you."

"You're welcome."

She ate, still organizing her thoughts. It was what she did, even when she had everything planned; going over and over every detail, making sure it was perfect. She liked when it all fit together but until she put her plan into action, it would roll around her mind like a marble in a funnel. She supposed it was a little OCD of her, but it worked. Why mess with it? Her mother had always said, "If it ain't broke, don't fix it." Seemed to apply to nearly everything. Nearly.

When the waitress stopped by her table to see if she needed more coffee, she said, "Cindy." Pause. "Do you have a minute for a question?"

The waitress looked a little surprised. "Sure. Is something wrong with your sandwich?"

"Oh, no. It's great, thanks. I was hoping you could tell me something."

Cindy waited, a little confused. "I can try." She stood a little closer to Amanda, waiting for her to continue.

"I was wondering if you could tell me anything about the tragedy that happened in town a few years ago."

Cindy stiffened. "Tragedy?"

"The murder. Over on Ridley."

"I'm sorry. I have no comment on that matter. Would you like more coffee?" her smile was a little forced, a little uncomfortable.

"Yes, thanks," she paused and, when Cindy leaned forward to pour, she said, "I'm not a reporter. Here, my card." She slid her Out of the Dark business card over to the edge of the table. Cindy glanced at it. "I swear. I'm not a reporter."

Cindy nodded. "Okay, but I don't know what I could tell you that wasn't in all the papers."

"Actually, I'm looking for someone who might be able to help me."

Cindy shifted her weight to her other foot and eyed her thoughtfully, head slightly to the side.

"I'm trying to find Jack Barnes' girlfriend at the time."

"And you're not a reporter?" Cindy's voice held a tone of disbelief.

Amanda shook her head. "Absolutely not. My team has been called in to research the house and I thought she might be able to give me a little information that I wouldn't have access to otherwise. Truly. I don't even have her name; I only know she worked here."

Cindy thought for a moment and asked, "Is there anything else you'd like? Some dessert? Or should I bring the check?"

Amanda sighed. She had a hard time hiding her disappointment, but respected Cindy's apparent decision. Always professional, always respectful. It was the only way to be. "Just the check, thanks."

Cindy walked away and Amanda stirred her coffee. Ah, well. These things happened sometimes. Maybe she could turn something up in her research. She hoped that Dom and Brian would have a better time going through the storage unit. She looked up when she heard footsteps stop beside her table, ready to thank Cindy as she took her check, but it was the hostess who greeted her. The woman sat on the bench across from her.

"What can I do for you?" Her name tag read Laurel.

With renewed hope, Amanda sat up straight. "My name is Amanda Harper and I work with a team that was called in to research Jack Barnes' house. A paranormal team. I was hoping someone here could put me in touch with Barnes' girlfriend at the time of his murder," she said quietly.

Laurel seemed to be sizing her up. Finally, she reached out her hand to Amanda. "Laurel Stewart. Nice to meet you."

Amanda shook her hand as realization spread across her face. "Nice to meet you." They sat in one of those "what do I say next" awkward silences. Amanda smoothed out the napkin on her lap and folded it under her plate. She leaned forward onto her arms.

"Well, you're definitely not a reporter," Laurel said with a slight smile.

"I take that as a compliment," Amanda responded. She grinned and Laurel relaxed. A little. The ice was broken and each had a bit of more an idea of the other.

"I don't know how I can help you. I wasn't there when it happened."

"I'm really wanting to know more about the man himself as opposed to the…" she fumbled for the best word. "I am sincerely sorry for your loss."

Laurel glanced at the table for a second, then back up meeting Amanda's eyes. "Thank you."

The quiet grew around them until Laurel said, "The man himself was amazing." She hesitated, slightly. "Jack Barnes was intelligent and kind. Funny and sweet. We only dated for a few weeks, but I could have spent the rest of my life with him."

Amanda's heart went out to her. It had been two years since, but she could see the love in Laurel's eyes. "And he liked cats."

Laurel looked amused but confused. "Excuse me?"

"I met up with one of the regulars on his bus route. A sweet little old lady…"

"With a big hat. Mabel."

"Yes! She didn't say a lot but what she told me, she meant," Amanda smiled. "And she said Jack liked cats. Made me write it down."

"Oh, yes. I met her once, as well. She was a favorite of Jack's, and he did adore his cat. Caesar," Laurel sighed. "Yours is a paranormal team?"

"Yes."

"You're investigating his house?"

Amanda nodded.

"Seems fitting, I guess. He would have been excited himself to investigate a house with that type of…history."

"Do you think that…" Amanda's voice trailed off. Again. She had interviewed people before, she had researched and asked questions, and never had this problem before. "Do you believe…"

"That Park did it?" Laurel filled in.

Amanda nodded, almost relieved that Laurel had finished her sentence, and slightly embarrassed that she had to. She ran her fingers along the spoon on her plate, absently tracing its edge over and over.

Laurel shook her head. "Park didn't do it." There was a finality to her voice. As if handing down a truth from on high. "He was framed."

"By?"

Laurel sat back in the booth and half smiled, but not a happy one. "I don't know."

"Do you think it was paranormal?"

It was Laurel's turn to trace the edge of the table. She looked out the window at the parking lot. A mom was helping four kids out of her SUV. They were dressed in soccer uniforms and headed into the restaurant.

"That was Jack's area, not mine. He loved the paranormal. Investigating. We didn't talk a lot about ghosts and things that go bump in the night. Here and there. I don't even know how much I had thought about the paranormal before all of this. But I believe he tangled with something that he couldn't control. It wasn't Park. They were best friends. Inseparable. Park was destroyed when Jack died." Laurel leaned forward, her voice going lower. "I went to see Park in prison once the trial was over. After he was sentenced and all. I don't care whatever journal they said they found," she locked eyes with Amanda. "That man was innocent."

Amanda nodded. Laurel absolutely believed what she was telling her, but she needed more about Jack. "What about Jack's demeanor prior to the murder? Was there anything different in his personality? Anything that seemed unusual for him?"

"Not when he was around me," she smiled. "He did have the flu the week before he died, but everyone gets sick sometimes. He was great. That's all I can tell you. I don't think I'll ever meet another man like him and I don't really want to." She gave Amanda a sad smile. "I don't know if any of this helped you, but I do need to get back to work. Unless you have something specific?"

"Oh, no. Thank you so much. I appreciate you taking this time with me." She stood as Laurel got up from the booth.

She took her business card off the table to hand to Laurel, but Laurel gently pushed her hand back. "I stay away from everything paranormal. At least for now."

"I understand," Amanda said, "but I'd like you to take it. In case you ever need… anything."

Laurel nodded and took the card. She stared for a moment at the Out of the Dark logo and absently tucked the card into the pocket of her slacks. "You know…"

"Yes?"

"You may find this strange, but…off and on I swear I can feel Jack around me. Kind of watching over me." She shrugged it off, nervously.

"I don't find it strange at all. I'm sure he is."

Laurel walked away as Amanda called after her. "Thank you, again." She gathered her bag and sunglasses, picked up the check and went to pay the cashier.

"How was everything?" The cashier was obviously wondering what was up that Amanda and Laurel had spent so much time in conversation.

"It was great, thanks! I'll definitely be coming back." She gave her most winning smile as she took her change. It faded as she walked out to her car. "Mission accomplished," she said to herself. "Sad mission accomplished."

Amanda sat for a minute in VW Vinnie, putting the next address into her GPS and then texting her brother. *Done at the restaurant and will meet you at 11 Ridley.* She didn't want for a response. Brian was one of those people who never felt the need to answer unless he was asked a question, and even that was iffy. He couldn't even be bothered to type a "K," a pet peeve of hers. He'd either be at the Barnes house or he wouldn't. She'd call if she needed him. Or text Dom.

The GPS stated, "You have arrived," as she made her way down the dead-end street that was Ridley Road. "No kidding," she said under her breath. She turned into the short driveway beside the house and turned off Vinnie. "This is definitely the place." The boys weren't there yet. She got out of the car and leaned on it, staring at the house and lawn. She would have loved to walk around, gotten the feel of it, but she preferred to err on the side of caution. Not her town, not her house and alone at the end of an empty road. She'd stick close to Vinnie until the guys arrived.

Getting her camera out of the trunk, she took a few exterior shots of the house, from the carport side. She smiled and walked a few feet away from Vinnie to get a better view of the back yard. A cat was on a rock at the far end, staring at her. "Hey, kitty kitty," she called. She held out her hand and squatted down. "You're such a pretty kitty." The cat didn't move. Amanda took a few steps closer, staying on the asphalt of the driveway. She thought for a moment. What did Laurel say? Jack had had a cat named… Caesar? It was worth a try.

"Caesar, come here, pretty kitty. Come on, Cees." The cat cocked his head. He seemed ready to take a step toward her, but then heard a car pull into the driveway. He sprinted into the woods behind the house. "Damn. It's got to be him." She was a sucker for animals and, if this was Jack's cat, he'd been living outside and alone for a couple of years now. Was he keeping some sort of vigil, missing his owner, not understanding what had happened to him? To his house? The thought made her sad and she wanted to connect with him even more.

"Hey, Sis, whatcha doing?" Brian got out of the van and slammed the door.

"Quiet, Bri. I was trying to get that cat."

He rolled his eyes. "What cat? You're always messing with strays, sheesh, Ammie."

"He's Barnes' cat. I'm sure of it."

"Barnes? No way. It's gotta be some stray hanging around, looking for snacks."

"Nope. You're wrong. I know it."

He quit trying. He knew better than to argue with her. His sister was as stubborn as she was smart and it wasn't worth it. Dom got out of the van.

"How'd it go at the restaurant? Find anything?"

Amanda brightened immediately. "I found his girlfriend."

"Are you kidding? No way!" Brian chimed in.

They walked over to where she was standing. "Yeah. We had a nice chat. Got a little more of an idea of the guy Barnes was. So far, everything points to him being pretty stable, happy. She swore that Davies was innocent, too."

"Gets more intriguing by the minute."

They stood, looking up at the house. Amanda was concentrating on the woods when the realtor pulled up. "And," she said, "The cat's name is Caesar."

10

What a shitty day. The owners must've called at least five times and for what? Yes, the bills had been paid; the contractors had finished; paperwork had been sent to the accountants and he was talking to prospective renters. So what if he didn't get to his desk till nearly 11:30 every morning? Everything got done. Gimme a break! Every ten minutes they were on his ass. Didn't they trust him? Didn't they think he was doing his job? He was losing it. Pacing around his office like a caged animal in a zoo. The owners staring at him through the glass, pointing. Scrutinizing his every move as the walls closed in. He fumed. Fucking hell!

That was it. He had hit his boiling point. The last straw and he definitely needed to let off some steam. His eyes darted around his office like a bee trapped in the rear window of a hot car. Landing here, there, with a constant buzz in his ears. He took a deep breath, letting it out slowly like in one of those meditation commercials. "Become one with the bee," he smirked. The temperature dropped around him. "Become dead like the bee."

Joe grabbed his sunglasses. Rudy's was cool and inviting and so was that waitress. He smiled at the thought. Yeah, that waitress.

Someone had fired up the juke box with a little Credence Clearwater Revival just as he walked in. *I see a bad moon a-rising* droned from a back wall. Well, it was better than that '90's shit they usually had going. He was sick of boy bands who had no idea what real music was. Real music. Throw him some Slipknot or Metallica, he'd be fine. Happy as a pig in shit. He walked up to the bar and ordered whatever was on tap. Keep 'em coming. Turning around, he leaned on the counter with one elbow, looking for that cute little waitress.

He spied her toward the back of the pool room, setting some baskets of nachos on a table. As she maneuvered toward the bar, he stepped in front of her. "Hello, little lady," he said. Her name tag read Tina.

"Well, hello! Back from the other night? Is your friend here, too?" she asked. She lowered her tray.

"No, he couldn't make it. I'm alone."

"Oh, that's too bad. Hanging at the bar or getting some dinner?"

"Getting some dinner with you tonight," he said.

She smiled. "Just serving it, hon." She moved to walk past him and, again, he stopped her.

"You can serve me anytime."

She gave an uncomfortable half smile and stepped around him to go back to the kitchen. Joe settled onto a bar stool, pointing at the bartender and then to his empty glass. Yeah, he'd hang for a while. Maybe Tina'd be friendlier when she got off her shift.

"Hey, Buddy," he said. "Got any aspirin? Tylenol? Something?" The bartender put up his hands and shook his head. "Thanks, anyway." Damn. A nagging ache had settled in his temples and was leeching down the back of his neck. Maybe it had something to do with his concussion. Fuck if he knew. All the doc had told him was to ride it out. Rest. Whatever. He was probably dying, not that anyone would notice if he disappeared off the face of the earth. He took his beer and walked over to watch the guys playing pool. The throbbing in his head wasn't quite in sync with the rhythm of the music from the speakers above him. He leaned against the wall, cracked his neck and stared out into the crowd.

A figure caught his eye and it wasn't Tina's. It was tall and dark. Taller than the rest and it slid along the back wall in and out of the shadows and his vision. How could it be inside him and across the room at the same time? The familiar knot in his stomach tightened and tried to force the beer back up his throat. Joe put his arm out to steady himself, beads of sweat breaking out on his forehead. The volume of the music and the smoky air were making his head swim.

"You okay, buddy?"

He glanced out into the mass of people; eating, drinking, talking people. Unaware. The shadow was gone.

"You need a doctor? Let's get you outside to some fresh air."

Joe put up his hand to stop the guy. "I'm all right." He stood a little straighter. "Really. Just got a little dizzy. I'm fine."

The guy backed off and returned to his pool game. Joe gathered himself, pretended to be interested in the balls thudding across the green table in front of him. He searched the crowd in short glimpses, afraid to see what he thought had been there. What was keeping an eye on him. Maybe he did need some outside air. Maybe he should just go home. He set his beer on the table beside him. Cool air engulfed him.

I make the decisions here, Joe

A bone piercing cold settled into him, moving from his extremities to his core. A second consciousness flexed deep within his mind and the last thing he saw was Tina walking in, bringing another round of nachos to the table of guys playing pool. Joe, but not Joe, eyed her hungrily.

"Tina, honey. Grab me another beer from the bar?"

A brief nod and she was gone. He watched her ass make its way through the crowd. It was equaled only by her tits. Damn, she was hot. He swallowed the last mouthful in his glass and waited for her to return. Moments later he had a tall one and she picked up the empty. He pressed a five-dollar bill into her hand, holding it tightly, his other hand resting across his fly.

"I've got a tip for you, honey."

She tugged her hand away. "I'm sure it's not big enough."

He chuckled. "Playing hard to get?"

"Not playing," she walked back to the bar.

He nursed his beer, had another, and watched her. His headache there but duller now. She moved around the tables smoothly, joking and laughing with the regulars. Her smile was delightful. The black Rudy's Bar tee shirt accentuated her curves perfectly. He wondered what it'd look like wet. And off. He kept his eyes on her, obviously, but hidden behind his sunglasses. Every so often she would glance in his direction. He knew he was making her uncomfortable, a little nervous, and it felt good. He loved being in control and he fed off her uneasiness.

At 10:00 p.m. he walked outside and stood in the shadows beside his truck, waiting. Watching the doors to the bar. It didn't matter how long it took. He would wait until morning if he had to. Hell, he didn't HAVE to be at work at any set time, now did he? If he wanted to sleep in, he'd sleep in. If he wanted to bring this woman home and fuck her all night, he would. A newfound energy flowed through his body like electricity through a wire and someone, something, just threw the switch.

Around 11:30 p.m., he heard someone call out "goodbye" and Tina stepped through the door. She looked up and down the street as he slid up beside her.

"Well, now, little lady," he said. "Need a ride?"

She looked startled, and could that be a little fear in her eyes? There was a scent to her discomfort and he drew it into his lungs like a drowning man on his last gasp for life. Energy pulsed through him.

"No, thanks. I have one coming." She avoided his eyes and looked up the street again, trying not to notice him beside her.

"I'd be more than happy to take you anywhere. My truck is right around the corner."

She shook her head. "No, that's okay. My boyfriend will be here any second."

He took her by the arm, grasping it firmly enough that she couldn't pull it away. "Why don't you be a good girl and come with me?" he said. "I know a quiet place where we can be alone."

She planted her feet and tried to pull his hand off her arm. "Look, I'm not interested and if you don't let go, I'm going to scream."

He smiled. "Go for it, baby," and pulled her closer.

A hand came down on his shoulder and he was yanked backward. "Get your mother fucking hands off her." The guy was big, at least six feet tall. "Go to the car, Tina. I've got this."

Joe pushed him. "Maybe you better watch your woman. She was coming on to me all night."

The guy came swinging. He nailed Joe in the jaw, spinning him to the ground like you see in the movies. Joe laid on the pavement, the ache in his mouth throbbing almost more than his head. He pushed up on his arms and stopped. Lightheaded.

"Stay the hell away from her, man. I'll leave you a bloody pulp if you come near this bar again." He climbed into his car and left.

Joe stood. Anger flooded him. The jerk slammed him pretty good. He touched his jaw. The asshole would probably get his cock waxed pretty well tonight for stepping in like some fucking hero. To hell with that cunt. He didn't need her sorry ass. He punched his truck before getting in, denting the door panel. His knuckles burned as he gripped the door handle, echoing the new pain growing in his face. He hoped to God he didn't get a DUI going home.

He dreamed that night. He knew it was a dream because Tina was in his arms. He held her, her long chestnut hair against his chest. Her tits barely restrained by her tee. He massaged her shoulders, sliding his hands to the small of her back and pulling her close. Breathing in her scent made him hard. Harder. His mouth found hers. Gently at first, then hungrily. Pulling off her shirt, he kissed her neck and she moaned slightly. "Good girl," he whispered.

His hands found her breasts and he rolled her nipples in his fingers before moving to his mouth. She arched her back, pressing into him. His cock was on fire. He laid her gently in his bed, one hand sliding between her legs. She was wet. Dripping for him, and he ran a finger along her clit. She spread her legs in anticipation, needing him. Needing *him*. It didn't matter that it was a dream. He got lost in her scent. He'd have her the way he should have had her at the bar. His fingers found her pussy and he slid them in, the silky slipperiness made her groan. He rubbed her clit a little harder, then stood back and used his cock to tease her. Running it up and down, enjoying her wetness, knowing he was driving her to the edge. She gripped his ass, trying to pull him into her, touching his cock, his balls.

"Do you want it, baby?"

"Yes, please…"

"What do you want? Tell me."

"You. Your cock."

"Tell me where."

She bit her lip and glanced away.

"Tell me," he pushed his tip into her pussy, just a bit, and stopped. She pleaded with her eyes.

"In me."

He pushed in a little farther, feeling her grip him from the inside. He pulled out.

"Tell me."

"Inside me…"

He smiled and pushed in a little farther. "Good girl. Now tell me you're a cock tease."

"What?"

"Say you're a cock tease. You're a slut. You're a dirty little whore who picks up men and plays cock games. Say it." He took her wrists in his hand, gripping them tightly behind her until she grimaced, and leaned in to her face. He shoved his cock in a little deeper. She moaned, arching to take more of him in. He pulled back again. "Say it now, you slut." He slapped her face.

She looked stunned and tried to get away. He held her in place, talking an inch from her lips. "Say it."

"Let me go."

"Tell me NOW." He slapped her again, a little harder, and plunged his cock into her, as deeply as he could. She gasped and groaned. "Say it." He wasn't playing; his eyes were dark with loathing and he couldn't stand her face anymore. He only wanted to cum and get rid of her. She disgusted him. As much as he had wanted her earlier, he hated her now. Raising his hand above her head, she relented.

"I'm a cock tease," she said. "I'm a whore." It turned him on and he pounded her, plunging into her pussy over and over, ignoring her groans and pleas. The strength and control dizzied him. Angry sex. He fucked her like his life depended on it, and, at that moment, it felt like it did. He glanced to the side of the room. Her boyfriend was tied to a chair, gagged, and watching. Hah! Served him right to see his woman done by a real man. None of that shit he had pulled on the sidewalk earlier.

"Take it, bitch," he whispered in her ear as he wrapped his hands around her ass cheeks and pulled them higher. He put his hands on the backs of her thighs, her heels above her head. As hot and sweaty as he was, his hands were cool. Cold. And covered in shadow. No, that wasn't it. They were shadow hands, dark and cold. Feeling took over and nothing else mattered. He dove deeper. She let out a yell and a whimper when his body went tight and he exploded into her. His cum mixed with her juices and he leaned into her, cock still throbbing. Pulling out, he tossed her a towel. "Clean yourself up and get out. I'll leave a fiver on the nightstand." He rocked it. Fuckin' A. The little bitch had it coming. Admitted being a cock tease. Hah!

He stood in front of her and her eyes were on his cock. He looked down. What the fuck? He was small. Tiny. Like two inches,

What had she done to him? He reached down in disbelief as she started to laugh.

"I didn't feel a damn thing, you asshole."

He was in shock and didn't register what she was saying.

"How do you even pee with that thing, let alone pleasure a woman? Even if I was a cock tease, there'd be no point in wasting my time on that little thing. You're not a show-er, not a grower and definitely not a man. Your cum wouldn't fill a thimble! Do you even have balls? Do you jerk off with two fingers?"

Her words echoed in his ears. He was embarrassed, ashamed. And she kept on. Droned on. They circled his brain, driving his upset into anger, and his anger into rage. There was a voice from beyond him yet inside his mind.

Are you going to let her treat you like this?

He turned to her, eyes blazing. She was laughing and he was going to silence it. He backhanded her and she reeled onto the bed. He climbed over, straddling her, and grabbed a knife from his nightstand. For a second he wondered how it had gotten there, but the voice vibrated through him.

Now!

He plunged it into her throat. She made a few gurgling sounds and struggled but it was over quickly. "Bitch." He grabbed the towel he had tossed at her earlier and dropped it over her face. "Someone'll have to clean that up."

Turning to the boyfriend, he threw a massive punch to the guy's jaw. The chair tipped over and he landed on the floor, still tied. Joe kicked him in the stomach. "Next time, don't fuck with me," he sneered. He walked into the bathroom, catching a glimpse of a shadow behind him in the mirror. A dark shadow, maybe seven feet fall. Even in the dream he knew it was Black. Black's voice. Black's anger. Black's goddamn hands. He shuddered at the thought of some entity fucking through him.

He woke, caught up in that fear moment before he got his bearings. In his bed, in his room… It was creepy, but right now he had to pee. It was just a fucking dream anyway, right? The heaviness of the nightmare hung like a dark cloud over him as he stumbled to the toilet.

Morning came too soon and he rubbed his eyes. Still a headache, but maybe it was more from the booze than anything else. Hangover hard on, too. Hell. At least he wasn't two inches long. Strange dreams last night. Maybe that was from the beer, too. He made his way to the bathroom.   Why was he such an asshole last night? Could a concussion change your personality? He paused, fighting a wave of anxiety. Could a ghost? He sighed. Probably have that big guy and his friends gunning for his ass for days. He'd have to keep a low profile. Hopefully none of them would be looking for an apartment any time soon. That would be all he needed…a daily ass kicking. Well, he'd deserve it. He'd do the same if someone came on to his girlfriend like that. If he ever got another girlfriend.

He remembered the shadow from his dream and avoided looking at the mirror. It was that uneasy, not wanting to hang your heels over the side of the bed because something was going to grab you, feeling. *Only say Bloody Mary twice because the third time will take you to hell…* Well, he had to pee, but he definitely wouldn't with the baseball bat that was hanging between his legs. Turning on the shower, he stepped in. He leaned with one arm on the wall, wrapped the other hand around his cock and slowly stroked it till his cum was headed down the drain with his life.

Joe pulled the burn barrel across the parking lot to the side lawn.

It was a 55-gallon drum he had gotten years ago and used for burning the appliance boxes the crews left behind. It was easier than trying to set everything out for recycling and got rid of things a lot faster. Should do the trick today, too. He hoped. Joe stuffed the barrel full of cardboard, doused it with lighter fluid and struck a match. It whooshed to life and he caught a whiff of the smoke. Acrid and not quite like a charcoal grill. Hah. He could only imagine what would happen if he ate whatever got cooked over that fire. The flames grew and he wadded up some old newspaper, stuffing it quickly under the small branches he had thrown in. The area around the barrel got hotter. Those bizarre heat waves rose, pulsating the air above the flames.

Joe walked in to the main entrance of Forest View and came back with the board and planchette. He paused before the barrel. Not debating, really, but mustering up the courage to throw it in. Part of him, a small part, didn't want to let go. Didn't want to lose connection with the spirit world. Didn't want to give up the communication. It was comforting, somehow, even with the hell he had unleashed. He reached out and dropped the planchette in, the board itself still tucked under his arm. The flames spread for a second and then closed around it. He could smell the faint hint of plastic as the fire started to melt the planchette.

Crackles and pops, orange sparks rising with ash above the flames; it was time. He hesitated. The glow mesmerized him; distracted him. He broke his gaze away and wondered what faces he'd see while the board burned. Joe shivered and turned it over in his hands, looking at the letters, running his fingers over the cool grain of the wood, remembering the first time he used it.

He had been in charge of the crews that were working to transform New Castle Asylum into apartments. The building had stood so long, empty, as if it had been waiting to die. Like in those old horror movies when they finally shove a stake through the vampire's heart. It needed release. If they had demolished it completely, it probably would have fallen to dust in a quiet exhale of thanks. He had seen the board resting on the ground. It struck him as odd, as if someone had gently placed it there and walked away. The planchette was beside the board and he tossed them both into his truck while he finished work. And now, he knew, it had been waiting to be found. Waiting for him.

Days later, after stopping at the bar for a beer and heading home for a few more, it caught his eye. He had come out of the bathroom after a long, hard pee, and saw the board sticking out from the shelf. Huh. He was pretty sure he had it flush with the rest of the books and odds and ends he stored up there, but whatever. Maybe it had dislodged somehow. He picked it up, sliding a hand over the smooth wood. Cool, lacquered, with black painted letters. Placing the board on the kitchen table, he examined the planchette. Not so scary in person. The movies made them so much more…intimidating.

He looked around. Candles. Might as well set the mood. Didn't seem right trying to contact the dead under bright white fluorescent lights. He pawed through his junk drawer, knocking screws and a few pencils out of the way before finding a couple of little white votive candles. The ones that everybody has but never remembers where they came from. He lit one, letting the wax drip onto the lid of a Cool Whip container. Looking around, he grabbed a cereal bowl. At least it was better than a piece of plastic. He wanted to talk to the other side, not burn the house down. Joe smiled and switched off the kitchen light. If anyone had seen him, they would've thought he was crazy but what the hell. Not much else to do on a Friday night.

The room glowed with a soft flickering light. He stared into the flames for a minute, looking for the faces his buddy told him were always there. Nothing. He didn't put a lot of stock into those things, like staring into crystal balls to tell the future. He twisted off the top of the next beer and took a satisfying mouthful.

Joe placed his fingers on the planchette, resting them gently along its edge and let out a sigh. "Okay, okay," he said to himself, "What do I ask?" He sat for a minute. "Damn." It always happened that way. Have an entire conversation going in your head, only to go blank when you meet up with the person. Felt a little ridiculous, too, sitting there, waiting for something supernatural to happen.

"Is there, uh…is anyone here with me tonight?" Another swig of beer, but that took his fingers off the planchette. "Sorry," he glanced around. "Not sure if there's fucking rules to this thing."

Back in position, he waited. "Anybody around tonight? Any spirits who want to talk? Have a beer?" He shrugged. "Come on, do something," Joe stared at the board, trying to will something to happen. In the movies, the kids had to invite something in. Always ended badly, but movies weren't real, right? "All right, all you spirits out there. I invite you. Come! Talk to me. Let's have a party!"

For a split second he thought he felt a slight vibration; barely perceptible, like the tiniest of electric currents. Then it moved. The planchette circled the board, coming to rest on *Hello*.

"Holy shit," he sat upright. "Now we're talking." He would have smiled at the pun if he hadn't been so intent on the board in front of him. "Is this you?" Now that was a stupid question. "Are you a spirit?" Again, dumb question. It was either him moving it or it had to be a spirit. Still, a response came.

Yes

He was excited now. Even if it turned out to be his imagination and desire making the thing move, it was pretty cool. Would've even been worth the $9.99 price tag if he had picked one up at the store. Free entertainment tonight. Not bad.

"What to ask, what to ask," he hated when he blanked. "Are you male or female? No, wait. Yes-no is easier, right? Are you female?"

Another slight vibration, a slide.

No

"That's too bad," he chuckled. "Male, then. Okay." He wanted to grab another beer and sit back, take it all in, but he was sure you couldn't do that. Break the connection or something. This was too mind blowing to disturb what was working.

"What's your name? What should I call you?" There was a pause and then the letters came. Slowly, at first, then a little faster.

Black

"Black? Your name is Black?" The planchette slid directly to *Yes*. Shapes from the candlelight flickered across the wall. It was mesmerizing and everything else faded away for…he didn't know how long. Like when you get to work and don't remember the drive. At first, it was the dancing of the flames that took his attention. Next, a shadow formed on the edge of his vision. A man dressed in black with indistinct features approached him, hand extended. Dream-like. Fluid. He took it in his own without thinking and, as the long fingers closed around his, his first thought was to pull away. But he didn't. Couldn't. The entity's grip was powerful and chilling. Draining.

I think we'll work quite well together, Joe. I'll be your silent partner

The stranger shook Joe's hand and he was flooded with a fierce knowing. And fear. As if he had just met his unwanted destiny. The shadow man turned on his heel and was gone, and Joe was brought back to reality as the planchette sped out from under his fingertips to *Goodbye.*

"Goodbye? Are you kidding me? What the hell was that? Am I hallucinating now?" He nervously wiped his hand on his jeans as he tried a few more questions. No response. He sighed. His nerves calmed and the vision began to fade from his mind as he downed another beer. "Fine. Fine, Mr. Black. I guess the ball's in your court." He blew out the candle and tucked the board onto the shelf.

A branch cracked and he snapped back to the present. Drawing in a deep breath, the dry smoke burned his lungs. He coughed, eyes watering. That first night. In retrospect he wished he had known the rules. Like don't fucking touch the thing. But who knew? Who fucking knew that you could summon Satan's little brother with a toy you could buy from Walmart? He closed his eyes and exhaled, throwing the board into the flames before he breathed in once more.

Quickly turning, he walked toward the house and sat on a lawn chair beside a bucket of water and the hose. Hopefully he was far enough away that he wouldn't see the faces. Or let them see him.

After about fifteen minutes, Joe was surprised that a breeze kicked up. It had been still, birds singing, barrel burning, and now the leaves on the trees were turning their backs. His grandmother had always said there'd be rain when the leaves flipped over. But there was no rain in the forecast. He had checked that morning. Wanted to be certain before he began his evil deed; his last grasp at saving himself. Burning that board was seeing if he could throw himself a life preserver in an ocean of sharks. Going down for the third time and reaching… reaching…

The first drop hit his cheek. "Shit." The dark clouds had rolled in quickly and the sky went from day to night. He tossed the hose to the side and jogged for cover as the thunder rolled and the clouds opened up. Smoke billowed from the burn barrel as the storm put out the flames. Soon, there'd just be soggy ashes. At least he hoped that's all there would be. He'd check after the rain died down. If need be, he'd let it all dry out and spray the goddamned thing with lighter fluid, or gasoline for fuck's sake. Whatever it took. He went inside to watch as the heavens poured.

It was another nightmare. He knew it was a nightmare. Had to be. The room was dark and empty except for the chair he was sitting in. Dread. All he could feel was dread. What form of torment would it be this time? Why did it want him? He tried to move, to stand. He wanted to run but he was cemented to the wooden prison beneath him. There were no ties, no ropes binding him, why couldn't he move his arms? He struggled in his invisible confines until he heard it. Footsteps. Quiet, slow and steady. Coming his way. For that moment, his struggles stopped. His heart pounded and sweat was beading up on his forehead. A chant cycled through his head…this isn't real, this isn't real, this isn't real, this isn't…

A doorknob rattled. Clicked. Somewhere, on one of the four walls surrounding him, there was a door. He heard a slight creak as it opened. No dulling of the sound on a carpet; no, this dream wasn't friendly enough to have carpeting. Just a damp cement floor and dark gray walls. Probably rats somewhere, eagerly waiting to feast on his warm flesh. He waited for a single light bulb to come on above him…ah, but that would be in a crime drama, wouldn't it? Not a horror story. Not a living nightmare. The stench invaded the room. His stomach coiled and recoiled and he vomited across his lap. There was no embarrassment or concern, he was well aware how this would end. He just didn't know if he would be alive to see it.

Joe tried to force his eyes shut. Didn't want to see or know what was coming at him. Not feel the mind fuck he was going to get. The mental beating that would rival any physical one he could ever get and survive. Hah. Survival. Even if he could get out of whatever held him down, he knew he couldn't run. How do you outrun something that lives in your mind? Something that sleeps wrapped around your brain, breathing in your soul through your synapses? It was slowly sapping his strength, his will. Breathing in his life force and exhaling its own dark desires. And it hurt. He ached to get away.

It drew closer to him, inside and around him. It pulled him closer like an unwanted lover and sadistic animal trainer all in one. He had let it in, this he knew. Had given it access to his life, free reign to destroy all that was good or might have been. There was no chance now. No way to redeem himself, no way to escape this shit side of his fate. Joe leaned as far back as he could, like a child pressing deeper into a dental chair. Trying to slide away, knowing pain was inevitable. Drilling dry into his brain. Where was the fucking Novocain? There was no escape and his apprehension was palpable. It could be worse, and more cliché, if there was a leaking faucet somewhere near him, with its drip drip drip pushing him to the brink of insanity. But that would have been more kind. A ledge to drop off, to escape what lay just inside the darkness that was preying on his mind. Taunting his sensibilities. "Now this won't hurt a bit," as it dove in harder and the needles pierced his nerves.

He opened his mouth to scream. Nothing came. No sound, no gasp not even a desperate wheeze. A caricature of a horror movie reject, he sat there. Eyes wide. The need to scream, not to alert someone because no one could help him, but to let out the terror that had been rising like bile in the back of his throat. He wished someone would hear, would know. But that was impossible. It was inside him. Rolling around his brain. The nightmare was the fun of it all; the comic relief of what sat growing inside him. Hah. He could've wished for a tumor. At least it would die when it killed him. This thing would live on. Would find another soul to attach its tentacles to and suck dry.

Another breeze of decay and his stomach reeled. He retched, stomach muscles nearly tearing with the force, and a few strands of bile hit his knees. Drool dripped from the corner of his mouth and his nose ran. He panted for a moment, wishing he'd black out. Wanting to be comatose and free for a little while. Sleep didn't free him. Sleep was its playtime. Letting him know who was in control and what it could do with a blink of its eye. If it had eyes. He had seen a shadow moving around the house lately. It didn't even try to hide itself anymore. He closed his eyes, laying his head back. A tear would've slid down his face if he had any. He was dry. There were no more tears when you've resigned yourself to your fate. To its fate. He'd be giving in totally soon. Giving up. Living as a shell of a man, taking care of the dictates of some in-fucking-human black hearted thing. He hoped it would let him die someday.

The darkness circled him, slowly at first, then gaining speed. Around and around. Dizzying. It stopped and a face, lips drawn up in a grotesque mockery of his own, stared into his eyes. He could feel its breath on his cheeks, if you could call it breath. Septic steam, rotting refuse. By now his eyes should have been used to the darkness but that was part of it all, wasn't it? People fear the unseen. The unknown. And it wanted his fear. Lived for his terror. Its eyes moved down his neck to his chest and poured into him. Burrowed. His lungs fought to keep him breathing as cold blackness pumped through his arteries, flowed through his veins. His blood ran black and cold, numbing him. Absorbing him. As his eyes went black, he felt himself losing consciousness and he thanked God for that. Or something.

He woke drenched in cold sweat, pajamas sticking to his slick skin. Even the sheets were soaked. He rubbed a hand across his eyes and glanced at the clock. It was… well, it didn't matter what fucking time it was. He peeled off the wet clothes and grabbed a few towels from the bathroom, spreading them out on the bed. That'd work till morning when he'd change the sheets. He pulled up the comforter and tried to sleep. Like that was going to happen.

Eventually, a thin ray of sunlight crossed his pillow. He watched it, waiting. Hoping he'd doze off, give in to the hundreds of sheep he'd counted all night. Joe sighed. Might as well get up. The alarm would be going off in an hour anyway. He stood and stretched, then grabbed the towels and sheets from the bed. The shitty night's sleep was going to wreck the whole damn day. His head had that "you didn't sleep more than three hours" ache to it. Going into the bathroom, he grabbed the bottle of aspirin from the medicine cabinet. It rattled. Nearly empty. Fucking hell, he guessed it should be. He'd been eating them like candy lately. Choking back four, he turned on the water in the tub. Maybe a long soak would help him feel better.

He slid into the hot water, leaned against the cool porcelain, and flipped the faucet off with his foot when the water lapped at his shoulders. Joe rested his head on the edge of the tub and let his body go limp. The heat soaked into his muscles, making its way to his bones, and eased the tension from him. With every breath he fell closer to sleep. This was exactly what he needed. His thoughts drifted.

He was floating. Rising higher, to where the air was cool and he could see the town below him. It was night and street lamps lit the area, TV's glowed in living room windows. Up ahead was darkness. He was moving toward it, not flying but being pulled by an unseen force. Joe tried to wrestle away knowing that doom lay in the heart of the darkness, but he was like a dandelion in a dust storm. Weak, useless and facing total destruction. He approached, faster now, and could make out the apartment building…but not. Forest View was a crisp clean unit. This was different. It was the asylum. Abandoned, broken and terrifying. He was being pulled down, faster and faster, toward the building. He covered his face with his arms, waiting for the impact of the cement, but the roof and walls disintegrated as he fell far deeper. Before slamming into the embalming table in the morgue, he woke splashing and grabbing for the sides of the tub. The waves took moments to fade. "Shit," he laid back, rubbing his eyes, trying to compose himself. The water was much cooler now and uncomfortable. To hell with his bath. He stood, reaching for a towel. His balls felt as if they were trying to crawl into his belly. Hot, cold, sweat, chills. He wrapped a thick towel around his waist and stepped onto the mat in front of the sink.

Running a hand through his hair, he looked into the medicine cabinet mirror. He hadn't shaved in at least three days. Shaving was for men who had a life. Who went out into the world and dealt with people. Men who could see light at the end of whatever tunnel they were dealing with. Hell, the tunnel he was staring at had a rockslide behind him and a train barreling toward him. He threw the towel in a wad on the floor.

He walked into the bedroom figuring he'd grab a pair of jeans and a shirt when he noticed an odor. A burnt smell. That damp wood fire scent that lingers after you've dumped water on a campfire. Like when you were a kid using one of those old wood burning pens on a 4 x 6 block of wood. Damn it. Did he leave the window open yesterday? Without getting dressed he walked through his living room and office, pushing aside the thought of what it had once been. The small single window was closed…and he never opened the one in the bedroom. It was puzzling and the smell was stronger now. He'd have to figure it out after breakfast and then get some fans going to blow out the smell before any prospective tenants came for a tour. He unlocked his office door, and stuck his head out into the hallway. Nothing but clean, cool air. Stumped, he walked back to the kitchen and stopped dead in his tracks. There, on his kitchen table, was the Ouija board, looking as pristine as when he had thrown it into the barrel. Only the edges were smudged, as if they had touched something ashy.

He stared, stomach in a knot, shaking. A hand touched his shoulder. It could have been a comforting gesture by a friend except for the bone chilling cold that stabbed him like an ice pick and he whipped around. Nothing. He guessed Black was serious about keeping the conversation going. He guessed he was fucked.

11

Jay rolled down the window of his Corolla as Dom walked over. It was a dusty, older car with a "Roger's Realty" sign on the side. "Do you all want to hop in and I'll take you to the storage unit, or do you want to follow me?"

"Either way, whatever works better for you."

"I don't mind driving you over. I have to come this way to head home anyway, so it's fine."

"Okay, thanks," he hit the clicker that locked the van and they climbed into Jay's car. Dom in the passenger seat. Amanda and Brian were immediately in "Professional Investigation Mode" and didn't argue over who was going to sit where. There were no yells of, "Shotgun!" He smiled to himself.

"I brought some paperwork, in case you do find something you want. Everything's been listed and given a ballpark price to start at the auction. It hasn't been publicized yet, so I got a release form in case there is something that can help you with the investigation."

Dom nodded. "You have no idea how curious I am about what's in there. Anything that would give us some clue or an insight into Barnes…damn, what I wouldn't give for a smoking gun right about now."

"I'm sure. I just don't know if there's anything like that. It's mostly boxes of personal stuff, nothing I'd call too interesting. But I don't know what might be a spark for you."

They drove for a few miles making small talk about the weather, how it wouldn't be a "dark and stormy night" for their investigation. Amanda wished it would have been. It added to the creep factor, which she loved anyway, but the ozone and electricity from a good thunderstorm seemed to heighten her sensitivities. And the activity. Kind of added a buzz to the place.

On the edge of town, right before they would have picked up the highway home, Jay pulled into the Store It Urself lot. He drove through the long, orange buildings with large garage door openings. "Building 3, unit 35," he said as he parked in front of a nondescript door. They got out of his car and stood, looking around, as Jay found the key to unlock Barnes' unit. He dropped the lock into his pocket and pulled the door upward. It opened with an echoing metal grind.

There was furniture, neatly covered with plastic, and boxes, mostly labeled, stacked along the walls of the unit. "Who got the job of packing all these things up?" Dom asked.

"After the cleaners went through the scene and his brother signed off, the bank hired our firm to sell the house. It kind of fell to me. I hired some guys and oversaw it all. Not the most fun, but you do what you have to do. A lot of things went to Goodwill, his clothes and such."

Dom motioned toward the inside of the unit and Jay waved him in. "Be my guest. If you have any questions, I'm here." He leaned against his car and began thumbing through his phone.

Dom walked in, with Amanda and Brian at his heels. "Let's do this systematically," he said to them. "Take a box, look through, on to the next. I don't want to miss anything." Brian took the left wall; Amanda, the back. "With the three of us, it shouldn't take long."

The box labels were accurate; books, appliances, DVD's. They moved around the furniture that was stacked in the middle; a brown, overstuffed sofa, a matching recliner, a coffee table. The bedframe, mattress and box spring were wrapped in plastic and leaning against the back wall. Dom maneuvered around a big screen television that was next to a box of its accessories. Some crates were sitting on top of end tables. One was on top of a microwave oven.

"This guy liked to read," Brian said. "He's got a great collection here. Horror, supernatural, paranormal. Lovecraft, Poe, a lot of classics." He took them out of the box, one by one, then repacked them. One box done.

"Wow. Old VCR tapes here," Amanda added. "Same theme, though. Documentaries on the paranormal, old sci-fi and horror classics." It was the history of a life. Fascinating, but sad to all be boxed up to be dispersed. Or thrown away. "Bela Lugosi! I think I would've liked this guy."

Dom was quiet. He was going through some cardboard boxes of books, DVD's. So far nothing jumped out at him. He wasn't discouraged. Not yet. It was wild that they had access to it all. He pulled a box of DVD's off the microwave and set it on an end table. The guy liked his movies. He took a few off the top, setting them to the side, and reached into the bottom layer. Clear plastic CD cases. Maybe the guy liked to record his own. He pulled them out to read the handwritten labels. Then whistled. Brian and Amanda stopped what they were doing and looked at him.

"What? Find something?"

He turned it over in his hand, holding it up for them to see. A homemade CD in a plastic case, but it was the label that intrigued him. *October 16, 2016.* Within a month of the murder. There were other CD's with dates, but this one was the latest and last date in the series. It could have been music; they were in with pre-recorded albums, but something in him said this was more. Key. He took the handful of dated discs out of the box and set them aside.

They continued their search. More books, a lot of kitchen stuff. Dom didn't know why anyone would save that but maybe someone would want an old pizza cutter and some steak knives at auction. Or not. He chuckled. It was an odd assortment of things. If he had to clean out someone else's old house, he probably would have boxed everything, too.

They pretty much all finished at the same time. Amanda had her hands on her hips.

"Thoughts?" Dom asked.

"Done," came Amanda's reply. "I think we've been through every inch of every box."

"Oh, yeah," Brian said, "And more."

"Great," he picked up the small pile of homemade CD's. "Then let's get going." He walked out and showed the stack to Jay. "Are these on your list?"

Jay gave them a quick look through. "Music CD's?"

"Not sure," Dom replied.

"I can't charge you for CD's someone burned themselves. I didn't realize they were in with the store bought ones."

"I appreciate that. Maybe there's something on one of these that will help with the investigation."

"You think there's some sort of evidence on there?"

"I'm hoping."

"I was hoping for a dart board for my man cave," Brian said under his breath.

"You don't have a man cave," Amanda said. "You're lucky you have a bedroom."

"Someday, Ammie. Someday," he smiled.

They made their way past the boxes and furniture and back to Jay's car. Dom was waiting for them with the handful of CD's in his hands. He gave them to Brian, who immediately thumbed through, checking out each date. They piled into the Corolla.

"Once you're at the house, do you need me for anything?" Jay asked. "I can stay a little while, but have another appointment to get to." He started the car and drove the maze of storage buildings out to the main road. Deep down, he hoped they didn't need him for anything.

"I think we're set," Dom replied.

"Okay. I'll let you in, and then, when you're done, just lock the side door and pull it shut. That way we don't have to worry about dropping off the key somewhere and all that jazz."

"Okay, sounds good."

"How long do you think you'll be?"

"Every investigation is different. It depends on if there's activity, how the night goes. We're there till probably 3:00 or 4:00 a.m, probably."

Jay nodded. "I let the police station know you'd be there. With its history the house has had its fair share of visitors. People who want to peek into the windows, kids who've tried to break in to check it out."

"Thanks. Totally appreciated," Dom said. "It'd really put a crimp in the night to be pulled out by the police."

"Yeah, it would," Jay smiled.

Jay turned down the dead-end street and Amanda could see Barnes' house ahead. Brian was staring out the window, watching the scenery go by, but her eyes were fixed on 11 Ridley. She wasn't quite sure what feeling, if any, she was getting from the house, but there was definitely something that struck her. She thought, for a second, that she had seen a small girl in the back yard. A glimpse of a child with long hair and a short, pale dress. It was a flash and gone. It caught her eye because Caesar had jumped and ran when the little girl turned. Amanda shook her head. She wasn't accustomed to seeing ghosts, just sensing them.

"Did you guys see that?"

"What?" Brian asked.

Dom turned in the front seat and looked at her.

"Nothing." She left it at that. For now. She pulled her clipboard out of her purse and jotted it down. Whether it meant anything or not, she always kept notes of the things that were odd, unusual or otherworldly. Kind of her paranormal diary.

Jay parked behind Dom's van. "You know, you're welcome to come in, see the setup, get a feel for how we work."

"Thanks, but I think I'm better off going about my way. The paranormal leaves me up at night, afraid to look out my windows." They all laughed, even though on the inside, he meant it. He got out of the car, went up the side steps and unlocked the door. Dom shook his hand.

"Once we go through our findings, I'll give you a call. We can meet up and go over everything at that point."

Jay sighed. "And hopefully I'll be able to move this house after that."

Dom smiled. "Hopefully."

Jay left. Dom looked at Brian and Amanda, then went to the van, opening up the back doors. "Let's do this." They grabbed the equipment cases while Brian stopped at the passenger door to pull out the cooler, and met inside. Amanda put hers on the floor beside the kitchen table. She turned, taking it all in. The emotion of the tragedy sunk into her chest, bleeding into her bones. She shivered. Taking a couple of slow, deep breaths and exhaling, she tried to ease it. The feeling stayed, climbing farther up her spine, and she walked outside. Time to ground a little more, get centered, before dealing with the residual energy in that kitchen. Dom joined her. "You okay?"

"I will be. But the feeling in that kitchen, wow," she paused. "I'll be in in a few minutes."

"Okay." Dom went back inside. Brian had put the CD's from the storage unit on the kitchen table and had begun opening the cases.

"Where do you want to set up?"

"Let's move this table into the living room. I want some cameras out here and don't want us in the way."

Brian immediately took one end of the table while Dom picked up the other. They maneuvered past the equipment and through the archway into the living room.

"Right there's good." They set the table down not quite in the center of the room, a little way back toward the wall but with room to walk around to the other side. "I want the wall behind us, so we're facing into the room. "

Brian knew that without asking. Never have your back exposed, regardless of the situation. He brought the cases in while Dom unloaded a couple of folding chairs from the van. Amanda was still outside regaining her composure. She walked in behind Dom and continued past the kitchen into the living room.

"This house needs a cleansing," she said, unraveling camera cords. "The energy in that kitchen is really off."

"That's where Barnes was murdered."

"I figured. Had to be, the way it hit me."

Brian opened the laptop and turned it on. He plugged it into the wall. It was fully charged but they'd be leaving it on most of the night. Next, he plugged in a power strip. They'd have to run the DVR system; keep the walkie talkies charging, although it was a small enough house they probably didn't need them. A yell would suffice. He'd have them ready just in case. He took out the voice recorders and meters, arranging them on the table. The ghost box, motion sensors, the cameras; all were ready and waiting.

Dom took one of the walkies and snapped it onto his belt. Habit. It was good to have a few ways to communicate back to base. His phone was in his pocket on airplane mode. He didn't want any phone "pings" to interfere with the equipment they were using. Stray signals could cause false positives and inaccurate readings.

"Amanda, you're with me," he said. He scooped up a camera and walked into the bedroom. She followed behind him and held the camera as he opened the closet door. "Bri, can you bring in one of the chairs?"

"Yup. One sec." Brian came around the corner with the chair and handed it to Dom, who placed it inside the closet. He stepped onto it and positioned himself under the square board that covered the opening to the crawlspace. Placing his palms flat against the board, he gave it a test shove. It moved easily and he slid it out of the way.

"Wish we had a step ladder," he said. He was still about two feet short. "Bri, give me a boost." Brian locked his hands and Dom put one foot into them. He pulled himself up as he pushed off of Brian's hands and sat on the edge of the attic opening.

"Need a flashlight?" Amanda asked. She reached into her pocket and tossed it up to him.

"Yeah, thanks." He flipped it on.

Dom shined the light throughout the crawlspace. Dark, small and empty. There were beams, alternating with pink insulation, but that was it. There was no way anyone was walking around up there.

"This put the 'crawl' in crawlspace," he said down to his team. "The report is footsteps up here, and I don't see how a person could have done it. I want a camera and voice recorder up here." Brian stepped onto the chair and handed Dom the camera, unwinding the cord as Dom positioned it for the best field of view. Amanda went back to base camp to check the feed.

She turned on her walkie talkie and held down the talk button. "Face it a little more to the left," she said to Dom. She let the button out and it gave its usual annoying beep.

She could hear Dom fumbling with the one on his belt and she smiled. The camera view of the crawlspace changed on the monitor, allowing her to see more of the attic.

"How's that angle?" he asked, again the squelch of static and beep.

"Much better."

"Good."

She could hear them talking without the walkie talkie. It was such a small house and the sound carried. Not that it had to, since they were only separated by a doorway.

"I'll bring you a voice recorder, hang on," Brian said. He came back around the corner and grabbed one off the table, winking at Amanda.

Dom rested the recorder on a beam, turned it on and lowered

himself through to the chair in the closet. He left the opening uncovered and hopped down.

"Next?"

"Let's get cameras going in the kitchen. I want one pointed directly at the center of the floor, where Barnes was found, and one focused on the basement door." Amanda was already unraveling the cords when they walked into the living room. Brian picked up two cameras while Amanda juggled their wires. As careful as they were when putting away the equipment, somehow camera wires were like Christmas lights. Tangled. Brian took one end and walked into the kitchen, Amanda in tow. She paused, her demeanor dropping for a moment.

"You okay?" Dom asked.

She gave a quick, unconvincing nod. "I am. The energy here is…draining. It's like despair. Despair and confusion. Terror." She shook her head, as if to shake off the feeling. "Poor guy."

"You're gonna be all right?"

"Yeah, I will be. Just need to take this spot in small doses."

"You got it. Why don't take a turn at base?"

Again, a nod. "We've got to get to a point where we can run base camp from the van and be separate from the investigation site."

"Yeah, you're absolutely right. But for now…"

"We're stuck," she smiled.

"Yup." Dom wished he could help her out. He'd love to be able to monitor from outside and keep the residence entirely investigative. "We'll get these cameras set and then check out the basement."

"And then some dinner?" Brian asked hopefully.

Amanda rolled her eyes. "Really, Bri? We should call you Shaggy. Get a mascot named Scooby Doo." She turned and walked back into the living room.

Dom took one of the cameras and spied out some areas where he could attach it. He found a hook in the wall over the kitchen table area. It must've been used for a clock or something. Maybe a painting. It was off center on the wall, closer to the side door, but it'd work. He could get a good focus, directly on the spot where Barnes died. He attached the camera to the hook, made sure it was secure and called to Amanda. Static, beep.

"How's it look? I want the middle section of the kitchen floor, near the cabinets."

"Yeah, I think I know the spot… it needs to angle downward a fraction more… there. You've got it."

"Great," he said. "Brian, find a spot for that one so we can get the entire basement door. The reports are of it opening and closing. I want to be sure we can zoom in on the doorknob."

Brian jumped in and soon had camera three mounted on the counter, focused directly on the door. "How's that, Ammie?" he called.

"Perfect."

Dom peeked into the living room. "Ready for the basement? It's not much, but we should all be familiar before going dark later."

"Coming." She left the DVR monitor and followed Dom and Brian down the steps. It was as dank and musty as when he had walked through it with Jay. Brian was never one for dark, damp places and was already moving around as if cobwebs were attacking him. He brushed off the back of his neck.

Dom glanced at Amanda. "Anything down here?" He pulled the string to turn on the light. He loved having someone sensitive on the team. It gave them an idea of where there might be possible activity. Kind of brought in a focal point to add to whatever history they had dug up.

She looked around. "Not sure. It's hard to know what's still the feeling from the kitchen…if it's bled out to the rest of the house…or if there's something else. It's not bad down here, but the entire house doesn't feel 'right.'" She shivered as if a cool breeze went past her toward the steps.

"Should've brought your laundry, Ammie. Could've thrown it

in," Brian pointed to the washing machine.

"You're an idiot," she chuckled.

"You're the sister of an idiot, remember that," he laughed. "Okay, okay. Do we need a camera down here?"

"I don't think so, but it doesn't hurt to run one. Everything that we can record is good, even if it's extra hours of review," Dom offered.

"And you never know what you might catch," said Amanda with an evil grin.

"What? What did you pick up on? Ammie, did you feel something down here?" Brian questioned her as she went up the steps. "Come on, Ammie. Tell me. Are you pulling my leg?" Brian began brushing off the back of his neck again, turning around to see if something had touched him. He followed her into the kitchen. "You're messing with me, aren't you?" As much as Brian loved the paranormal, and was the best at tech and review, she could freak him out. He grew up with her knowing things she couldn't and, at times, she had made him crazy with it. On purpose. Sisterly psychic torture, he liked to call it. "Ammie!"

She ignored him and went to unwind more cord for the last video camera. She handed it to him and said, "Facing straight down the stairs."

"Now you're creeping me out," he said, but took the camera and got it mounted.

When everything was up and running with a live feed to the monitor in the living room, Dom unfolded a chair and sat down at base camp. He slid his laptop over in front of him and took the first CD off the pile. It was time to see what Barnes had recorded.

October 16, 2016. The drive whirred to life, bringing up a directory. It seems there were not only audio clips but video and still pics as well. "What have we got, Mr. Barnes?" Dom said absently. Amanda stood behind him while Brian sat down and pulled the cooler over with his foot.

"Start there," Amanda pointed at the picture files. "It might show us where he was and then we can see if the rest is worth going through."

"Good point," Dom clicked on the first group of pictures.

"Look at that place," said Brian. It was an imposing structure. The building itself had obviously been abandoned. Empty holes where windows should have been; ivy at one point had grown up the dull, reddish bricks. Now, it was brown, brittle and dead. The grounds around the building didn't look much better. It was as if this decrepit structure was placed in the middle of a hill and everything remotely close to it had crumbled and died.

"Are you sure this is the same date as the rest? It looks so…lifeless. It could be a winter shot and not October."

"They're all from the same date."

"It's got to be New Castle," Brian said. "Got to be…and damned if it doesn't look like the typical evil asylum. Taken right out of the movies, that one."

Dom cycled through the photos, one after another. They were all outdoor shots, different angles of the institution. Window shots, grounds photos. "If you ask me, this was where he started his investigation of the place. It's what I would have done…get a feel for the outside before going in. Especially window shots."

Amanda nodded. "God…look there," she pointed at the pic that Dom had clicked on. "Look at the window."

Dom zoomed in on the second-floor. There was an old, discolored curtain, and a shadow that covered part of it. "Are you kidding me?" It was there. Unmistakable. A dark mass in the shape of a man was standing at the second floor window.

"What a fucking capture," Brian said at close to a whisper. "But that thing doesn't look friendly."

"Can we mark it? That's definitely something I want to scrutinize. See if we can debunk it," Amanda stated.

"Yeah, I'll copy it to a file on my computer," Dom clicked

around, making a new folder for whatever they found that they wanted to revisit. He labeled it, "Barnes, October 16, 2016."

"Great," Amanda grabbed a folding chair for herself and moved in closer to the screen. "Keep going."

Picture after picture, they were finally inside the site with its decaying plaster, peeling paint and crumbling cement. Your typical abandoned asylum. Room after room of old, broken bedframes, half intact plumbing and forgotten laundry carts. Faded wallpaper in a dingy beige that must've been a yellow when it was new. Piss yellow. There wasn't much that would've made that place cheerful.

"Barnes kept great photographic notes, eh?"

"Yeah…cool, but not comfortable. This was the last place the guy investigated. Pretty creepy, if you ask me," Brian stated.

"Definitely creepy," Amanda added. "You know, we're probably going to end up there, right?"

Dom nodded in agreement. "Yeah. I don't think we can avoid that, even if we find nothing here. I think we're going to have to see what his findings were and that's going to be our next piece in the puzzle."

Dom clicked to the next photo and stopped. Dead stopped. They all stared. There, in a selfie shot, was a picture of Barnes in a doorway, taken from a mirror in the room. Now, not only did they meet the man that this all centered around, they saw the same black shadow behind him that had been in the second-floor window. Standing over Barnes' shoulder was a tall, black mass in the shape of a man.

"It's got to be like seven feet tall," Brian exhaled. "What the hell is that thing?"

"Mark it," Amanda said.

"Hell, yeah," Dom responded. He copied it to his personal folder.

"As much as I love this business, that doesn't look good at all. That thing has balls," Amanda added. She continued looking, from the shadow figure to Barnes, to the shadow figure. "He had no idea it was with him. Look how he's smiling."

"It's got to be the same shadow that was in the second floor window. Has to be," Brian said. Dom was already positioning the first photo side by side with this one.

"Fuck," Brian said.

"That's for sure," Dom leaned forward. They were the same. Size, shape…and, almost, intent. He couldn't put his finger on it, but it had…intent. Balls, as Amanda had said. It had balls. Like it knew it'd be in the picture and didn't care. Like it wanted to be seen.

"While you go through those, here," Brian handed Dom his USB. "Drag over some of those audio files. I'll start going through them."

Dom plugged the USB into his computer. It didn't take long for the audio clips to transfer. Brian opened his laptop and uploaded them. He drummed his fingers on the table and watched the monitor as Dom continued through the still pics. As soon as the bar hit 100%, Brian had his headphones on and was ready to go. He hit play on the first clip.

Miss, is your name Carla?
Yessss

He touched Dom's arm without removing the headset. "Nice class A EVP." It felt like a great find, but then, he should've expected it. He wasn't going through hours and hours of evidence and stumbling on a voice out of nowhere. Barnes had already done that and these were the gems he sectioned off for future reference.

Amanda took the headset off her brother and listened while he looped the clip for her. She nodded and handed it back. She liked standing behind the two men. Having access to all the evidence was like having her fingers on the pulse of the investigation. And that sucker was beating faster.

Brian hit play on the next clip. His jaw dropped a little, surprised, and he handed Amanda the headphones. "His name. It said his name."

She listened, intently, although it wasn't necessary. What came through was so clear and so exact.

Jaaaack

Where you might have been able to explain away or debunk the first, there was no questioning this. No debunking. No "air in the heating pipes" or "someone exhaled in such a way as to sound like that," or whatever straw you might try to grasp. This was Barnes' name. Drawn out in a long whisper, but definite. Whatever this was, it was intelligent and knew who was there.

"Wow," Amanda reacted. "That's so cool. Wonder if it's the shadow from the photos." She tapped Dom's shoulder but he shook his head. He didn't mind letting them go through the audio; he was totally absorbed by the photos and anxious to see the video clips. There was only one reason to clip videos. Evidence. Something moving, an object, a... shadow.

Play. The next audio clip rolled through Brian's headphones and he sat back, stunned. He stared at the screen and clicked stop. Amanda looked at him, brow furrowed. "What'd you hear?"

Not a lot shook him, but this recording came close. So close. Or maybe it did shake him, some, on the inside. Turned his stomach into a mass of knots that he wouldn't admit to but if they didn't untie, he wouldn't be eating again for a long, long time. He had heard crazy EVP's before, but when you tied it in to what happened to this Barnes guy... Well. It was nearly a smoking gun.

"Bri?"

He hit play again to be sure he heard it right, although he knew there was no mistaking it.

"Bri," she said again.

He handed her the headphones in silence. She put them over her ears and nodded for him to start it up.

I've got news for you. You're leaving. You're out. I'm going to close this board, close your access to this house. You don't need to be here. Oh, yeah. You can go to the light or back to New Castle, I don't give a fuck. But you're not staying here.

"Okay," Amanda said. "That's got to be Barnes." It was oddly chilling to hear the voice of the man who had been beaten to death not more than twenty-five feet from where they sat but that couldn't be why Brian was so...shocked?

"Wait for it."

You're fucked.

A low, man's voice, almost a growl, had responded to Barnes. Her eyes widened. She pulled the headphones off and let them drop to the table, as if she could distance herself from what she heard. Separate herself from that voice.

"Shit just got real," Brian said.

Dom quit what he was doing and looked at his teammates. Brian pulled the plug to his headphones out of the computer and hit play, turning up the volume as loud as it would go. He let the entire section play, then looped the response.

You're fucked   you're fucked   you're fucked   you're fucked

Dom hit stop. The silence grew around them, as if the room was slowly filling with a heaviness that none of them could breach. "Son of a bitch," he said quietly. "Let's hit the video."

Amanda positioned herself between, and slightly behind, Brian and Dom. Best seat in the house and she questioned if she truly wanted it. Needed it, though. In for a penny, in for a pound, her grandmother would say. And they were in and getting deeper by the minute. Dom cued up the video.

"Too bad there's no popcorn," Brian said. His lips pulled back in a tentative grin.

Amanda rolled her eyes. Leave it to him to try to break the ice but this lake was frozen two feet deep with no cracks. The first video clip started running and they all settled in like they were watching a movie where they already knew the ending but had to catch up on the plot.

"We're obviously in the asylum," Amanda stated. "But what's that room?"

From the angle, they could see a couple of large bins on wheels, and Barnes was sitting on the floor.

"Probably a laundry. It looks like," Dom said.

Barnes was conducting an EVP session and was asking typical questions… *Are you male, are you female, did you die here?* He asked the spirit to make the colored lights on his KII meter come on. Barnes seemed to be getting some consistent responses, light-wise, according to his reactions. From the angle the camera was placed, they couldn't see the KII itself.

"A shame he didn't have it in the shot," Brian said. It annoyed the hell out of him, being the tech guy, that the proof was just off screen.

"Sucks," Dom added.

They heard a whoosh and a bang, and Barnes exclaimed. *Hey! Treat the equipment nicely, please, Miss. It's not cheap.*

"Whoa. It must've slid and hit the wall or something. That would've been a prime capture if the damn camera was set better."

"Hopefully the rest will be," Dom said. He positioned the mouse over the next video clip and clicked. The morgue. With a slam that came out of nowhere.

"Sounds like a metal door banging shut. Nice echo in that place," Brian said.

"Pretty creepy," Amanda added.

"Frustrating. Another shot off-camera."

"Can't count on where activity will be, Bri."

"I know, I know…"

They ran through similar short clips, basement rooms, first floor, some EVP sessions that Barnes had had, sounds in the background but nothing too exciting. One clip had what seemed to be a dark shadow, not anything discernable, but a shadow that moved across the screen and was gone. It could have been anything but somehow they each figured it was more than that. There was too much activity going on to think that it wasn't. But… they still didn't want to jump to conclusions. A healthy dose of skepticism was necessary, even when the evidence pointed to… well…something.

Dom clicked the second to last clip. It was starting to get dark outside; they'd been working on these for a couple of hours now. As much as they had been excited to get started on the house, they were soaking up the essence of this man and what had gone on before his alleged attack. Dom knew he'd be headed to whatever was left of New Castle before this was over.

Barnes was on the third floor now and emerged from the hallway. You could hear the muffled footsteps before he came into camera view, the sound of broken bits of plaster crunching and sliding under his shoes. There was graffiti on the walls and there, in the center and main focus of the camera, was a pentagram carved into the floor. Black candles were positioned around it, with other items strewn across the floor.

"Is that a Ouija board under his arm?" Amanda asked. "Tell me it's not…"

He asked a few questions and was obviously getting cold. Colder… and decided to try the board to get some responses. As he continued, something hit him in the cheek. A piece of plaster? A pebble? Something thrown. He threatened kids he couldn't see, as if a few had quietly sneaked in to cause trouble. A growl came out of the darkness.

"Oh, this can't end well," Brian said under his breath. "It ca…" He didn't have time to finish the sentence.

Barnes grabbed his equipment and before he could turn to leave, something came from the darkness and slammed him into the wall.

Amanda gasped; they all jumped.

It held him there, against the wall, for what seemed like ages, and then let him fall into a ball onto the floor. He lay there, panting, the pain and terror evident. He scrambled, trying again to leave, when another blow came. Barnes fought to get to his feet and, holding his side, ran in the direction of the hallway.

The clip ended.

Dom let out a sigh. "I guess we know what got him."

"I knew it was bad, but seeing something like that… and it's not even the worst of it all…" Amanda had no words to finish her thought.

"We're here to document. Remember that. If anything, ANYTHING, escalates or feels wrong here, we leave," Dom reassured. He knew he didn't have to. They were all smart about the unknown and safety for the team was paramount. That was it. "Anyone can make that call and we all turn on our heels."

Brian and Amanda nodded.

"There's one video left and then we can get started here. Are we good?"

Amanda took a deep breath. She knew he was referencing her; Brian would go on regardless. She was pretty strong, and followed her sensitivities. "Hit play." She hoped it wouldn't be Barnes getting attacked again. She couldn't bear seeing someone hurt.

The video began.

"Oh, man," Brian exhaled. They were no longer watching events from New Castle. They were looking at a scene, not far off from where they were sitting. Barnes had a camera on the basement door in the kitchen. They waited.

The basement doorknob jiggled, then turned. The door opened.

"Nice capture!"

"There could be someone behind it, Bri. You can't see."

"You know there's not, Ammie."

"You know there could be. That's all you need to know."

"This is Barnes, we're talking about. Come on, Ammie. You know it as well as I do."

"Yeah, well…knowing and proving are two different things. All that proves is the door opened, not who or what did it." She knew, though. And she felt. She couldn't let go of their protocols and standards… but she knew.

"Hard ass," Brian smiled. She gave him nervous smile. A shadow crossed the table where they had been working and Amanda jumped.

"It's a cat," Dom whispered. "There, in the window."

"Wow, off my game, I guess," Amanda smiled, embarrassed. Dom put his hand on her shoulder and gave it a squeeze. "I'm pretty sure it's Barnes' cat." She walked over to the window and opened it a crack. "Caesar, come here kitty kitty."

The blue gray cat, already halfway across the carport, turned, its ears perked.

"Come on, Cees," she sighed.

"I think we need a break before diving into this investigation," Dom suggested. "Dinner?"

Brian was on it. "Oh, yeah!" He pulled the cooler over and opened it. "Sandwiches? Snacks?" Some food might help untie the knot in his stomach. For now.

12

He sat on the curb taking some long drags on his cigarette, watching the sun slide down below the horizon. Bats were out swooping for insects. Joe watched for a few minutes, not wanting to go inside. Alone. Never before did he feel so much like one of those bugs. Tiny and pursued. Hunted. Waiting to be consumed. A fly in a spider's web. He took a deep breath then let it out slowly, watching the smoke form and dissipate in the evening air.

He stretched his legs and flicked the ashes off the end of his cigarette. The stars would be coming out soon. No moon tonight, but it still wouldn't match the darkness inside his apartment. The entire basement had gone shades darker since Black moved in. Hah. Moved into his brain, that is. Not even paying rent. Joe put the butt out on the asphalt, anxiety twisting like worms in his stomach. A light came on at the far end of the second floor. He shut his eyes, sucking in his breath and trying to gather some resolve to go check it out. Turn it off and pretend to chase kids out of the building. Pretend there was a real, physical, this side of the veil reason the switch was flipped. His temples started to throb.

He walked inside, climbing the stairs to the second floor with feet of lead. It was coming on again. He could feel it. The air was heavy and his dread was transforming into anger. Black's anger. Tunnel vision took over and he trudged forward, making his way to where this hell began. Where those bastards did their incantations and summoned his undoing. Where Barnes had brought this thing further into the world of the living, giving it a taste for fear and flesh. His hands balled into fists and he screamed inside his mind. *Please, please don't let it happen again. God, make it stop.* No sound escaped his lips. It was like something clawing the inside of his skull. He squeezed his eyes so tightly shut he thought they'd bleed. He punched a wall. The pain pulsed from his knuckles into his wrist and it brought him to reality. Reality. That was a joke. He walked to the end of the hallway and flipped the switch. "Stop fucking with the lights, Black, you asshole."

Heart pounding, he paused, waiting to see if Black would respond. Retaliate. End his madness. All he felt was the growing anger inside him. His? Black's? They mixed together, a sick blending of shit. He hated the world right now. It had been against him since the day he was born and it was time to do something about it. Something flexed in his mind and sent a dark strength pulsing through his veins. An invincibility. Yeah, it was time. He jogged down to his apartment.

His wrist ached as he opened the door but the darkness in his mind muted anything he could've inflicted on himself. Grabbing one of the votive candles, he threw it against the wall, surprised at how satisfied he was when it shattered. He shoved the kitchen table against the wall. An old cup of coffee spilled and the Ouija board slid off, hitting the chair and landing on the floor. Pain spiked through his head and he fell to his knees, holding the seat of the chair and panting. Black was good at pain. Used it like a goddamned choke chain. Don't go too far, Joe. Yank. Don't think you'll ever get free. Yank yank. Reality was slipping away like a curtain coming down on a play, only he was the one being played. He was the actor, going through the motions of life. There was no living. It was all a series of flashbacks and fear, as if the door to hell had opened and he had one foot through.

He turned his truck onto the main street and gunned it, tires skidding and kicking up gravel. He didn't know where he was going. The accelerator read 50 before he was through the middle of town and he slowed, just slightly, at the onramp to the highway. The roads were no longer curved; he slid into the oncoming lane when the road turned with ease that astonished him. His foot pressed the accelerator a little closer to the floor. It scared him, but there was no stopping. Black had control. Again. At this point he was sure he could close his eyes and the thing inside would keep him on the road. But he couldn't. Adrenalin and fear kept his eyes wide open. Even nearly crashing didn't shut them. He wanted to see what killed him. Thank it with his last breath.

The oncoming headlights became a blur and the blaring horns resulted in his middle finger thrust high and hard without a turn of his head. He was sure he caught a glimpse of one car swerving to the side of the road, missing the guard rail. A twinge of guilt, but his eyes were glued to the road rolling out ahead of him. The anger was quickly becoming his own, replacing the fear which had tightened around his heart and made his stomach turn. The car ahead of him, doing the speed limit, irritated him. He slid side to side, trying to get a spot to pass, and finally ground the accelerator to the floor and whipped into the oncoming lane. Pulling the wheel hard to the right he was in front of the asshole and slammed on the brakes. Screeching tires and the other car's bumper missed his by inches. He smirked. Served the bastard right. Don't fuck with him.

Towns went by, but he only saw the green of the highway signs. When Centerville was a quarter mile away, he moved into the exit lane and took the ramp at 50 mph. He smiled when the car held four wheels on the ground and wondered if he could've made the turn on two. Barely slowing at the stop sign, he crossed four lanes straight into a Home Depot parking lot. There were minutes until it closed but what he needed wouldn't take long. Supplies. A few supplies to get him through the night. He took the sunglasses off the neckline of his shirt, put them on and strode into the store.

He placed his things on the conveyor belt in front of the checkout girl. She tucked a lock of stray hair behind her ear and slid his first item across the scanner without looking up. Duct tape, garbage bags, zip ties. Beep beep beep, she hit the total button on the touch screen.

"Gotta hide a body," he said, dropping a twenty on the belt.

She nodded before the words had sunk in. Her eyes met his sunglasses instead of his eyes, her reflection distorted. "Good luck with that," she said.

He grabbed his bag and confidently walked out of the store. "Dumb fucks," he muttered. Joe threw everything into the back seat and drove on.

The exit for Hilldale came quickly. Faster than he thought it would, but when you're maintaining 85 mph, the miles fly by. He jerked the wheel and took the exit, feeling the vehicle want to lift off the road. A left, a right, a couple of turns and he'd be at his destination. He knew a place. Didn't know how he knew, but that didn't matter. It'd work.

Joe parked his truck at the far end of the apartment complex's lot, close enough to be accessible, but away from the brightest of the overhead lights. By the trees. Discretion was key. He sat for a moment, surveying the walkways and sliding on an old pair of work gloves he kept for dirty work, before grabbing the bag beside him. He let the door close with its usual thud and nodded to a couple walking toward the next building. Casual, friendly. With a calculating death in his eyes they couldn't see behind their reflections.

He walked determinedly down the running path a short way before cutting into the bushes. Sliding down a little embankment, he stopped in a small clearing. Big enough for a couple of deer to bed down, maybe be a fort for a kid or two. Just right for his purposes. He pulled out the duct tape and cut the end so the flap would be easy to grab, then settled back and got comfortable. It'd be a few hours before he needed it. Might as well relax.

The first runner's footsteps went by at 4:00 a.m. An early riser trying to fit in some exercise before hitting the grind of the day. Probably an accountant or IT guy, someone who would be sitting on his ass all day behind a computer screen. He despised the guy, sight unseen, and waited. Most of the people who ran this path, and there weren't many, would be hitting it after 5:45 a.m. He'd be done and gone by then. Long gone.

He recognized the next set of foot falls. Steady, sure. He knew but didn't know. Was familiar but had never met him. They'd meet soon, though. Joe shook his head. He hated this. Did he have the memory or was it Black's? Was a concussion slowly eating his brain or Black? Which thoughts were his anymore?

4:37 a.m. The next set of plodding footfalls. Heavier this time. More labored breathing. Either someone just starting their regimen or this fucker was on his way to a heart attack. Still waiting. It wouldn't be long now. His senses were heightened by the adrenalin starting to flow through his system. And then he heard it. The soft rhythmic sound of a woman's running shoe hitting the dirt. Almost like a pulse. It matched his heartbeat for a few steps, but his overtook it as the pounding grew louder in his head. He had to exhale quietly to bring it under control. A jaguar waiting for the right moment to strike.

His timing was precise. As her footsteps came around the slight bend above him, he bounded from below, catching her around the waist with one arm, the other hand over her mouth. He whirled them both over the edge of the path, rolling with her down into the clearing. Stunned for a second, her pause gave Joe time to grab the duct tape with his free hand while the other held her wrists securely behind her back. She had no time to yell before he had her mouth covered. He lay on top of her, still holding her wrists, while she struggled. Let her tire herself, the thing inside him said. Let her struggle herself weak.

She was fueled by adrenalin as he was, but his strength was

unwavering. For a fraction of a second, he recognized the terror in her eyes and felt Black's exhilaration grow. It was as if Black wanted to give him these glimpses to torture his soul. To show him who was really in control, who was calling the shots. A quick taunt of his sensibilities and Black shut him down once more.

She dug her heels into the dirt, trying to squirm from underneath him, but only succeeded in making small ruts under them. Her breathing was a pant now, if she had been able to open her mouth. The heaving of her breasts seduced him and he was rock hard from her struggling. He leaned his face close to her ear and whispered, "Keep it up, baby. It turns me on." She let out a small, fearful moan and tried to look into his eyes. Her own face was all that was reflected. He smoothed the hair away from her face and kissed her cheek. "Be a good girl and follow directions. Can you do that?"

She gave a quick nod, a tear running down her cheek. He kept her wrists tightly in one hand while the other found its way under her shirt. He grabbed her breast, causing what would've been a gasp but for the duct tape. Laughing, he shoved her tank top up so he could expose her. She arched her back to try to get away but it just gave him more access. He ripped off her bra and buried his face between her breasts. Another arch, another dig into the ground with her running shoes. Grabbing her jaw, and in a voice he didn't even recognize, he growled, "Try that again." She stopped. Limp. His nails had cut little half-moons into her cheek and blood had immediately welled up. She emanated fear. He slid his hand around to her back and let it slide to her ass, cupping one cheek and pulling her hips closer against him. He pressed into her, cock stiff and throbbing. She whimpered but didn't move. "You're learning," he said. He squeezed her wrists together and wrapped them in duct tape. "Just so we're clear."

Shoving his hand into the front of her shorts, past the lace of her underwear, he whispered, "Are you wet for me, baby?"

Black pulled away from Joe's mind and let him see exactly what he was doing. Repulsed from the vileness of his actions, he leaned back for a second and groaned. Black had made his point. He knew who was in command and who was the shit-shoveler. He pulled every bit of mental energy he had left and shoved himself off her. "Run," he spit out between clenched teeth. He yanked a pocket knife from his things and slashed the tape holding her hands.

She looked confused. Stunned. Terrified. "Run," he said again. "Before I fucking kill you." He sat on his knees, arms around his stomach, rocking. The girl scrambled, clawing her way up the embankment. He knew she'd be ripping off the duct tape and screaming once she realized she was truly free and he had to get out of there. He wanted to stay, let them catch him. Hell, even let them fucking castrate him. His life didn't matter anymore. But Black wasn't having it. He cut through the bushes, opposite to where the girl had run, until he came out on the far end of the parking lot. He heard her yelling in the background. Looking around, he got into his car, driving out of the lot as Black seeped around his mind, then drilled into him. The pain tore through his brain. Revenge would be exacted but at least it would be on him and not someone else. At least he saved this one, this time. He was sure he wouldn't get another chance. He knew he wouldn't. His mind was barely his anymore. As he got onto the highway, he thought about crashing his truck into a cement girder as he headed under a bridge. Instead, Black gripped the wheel.

Oh, I'm not done with you yet.

It echoed in his ears.

Joe was sprawled across his bed, still in his clothes. His head ached. Rubbing a hand across his eyes, he felt a sense of relief. Hah. Just a headache. A normal fucking headache. He sat up. His body was sore. Again. He glanced at the clock and was surprised to see it was afternoon. After-fucking-noon. There was some dried blood on his knuckles. He got up and went into the bathroom. His lip was cut and that's where he guessed the blood had come from. There was that hope, anyway. Memory was not his strong point lately and that scared him. Terrified him, really. The dark times were increasing in number; that thing sliding in and around his mind. Fuck. He had never believed in ghosts, let alone possession. It was almost easier to think he was losing his mind than to think something was taking him over. Maybe he had a tumor. He'd read about people doing crazy things, like climbing clock towers and taking aim at passersby. Tumors could do sick things to your brain. And that'd be his fucking preference.

He washed his face, peeled off his muddy clothes and got in the shower. Mud. Where the hell had he been? He stood under the steamy water letting it cleanse him. Wishing it'd wash his soul clean. The tears started and, before he knew it, he was standing under the pouring water with body wracking sobs; his hands balled into fists against the tile. How long he broke down was irrelevant. The water ran from cool to cold, but he stayed until the tears were gone. Chilled and spent, weak, he turned the off the faucet and reached for a towel. As he stepped onto the bath mat, he caught sight of his reflection in the medicine cabinet mirror. Older. He looked somehow older. The bags under his eyes spoke of restless nights and too much alcohol and the anonymous hell he was living.

He sat down on the toilet, head in his hands. Thinking. Not thinking. His sanity was slipping away like sand through his fingers. He pushed the thought aside and stood. Work. He needed to get to his fucking desk and get something done. Try to hide in paperwork and phone calls.

He rearranged apartment applications, dodged phone calls and found himself pacing. There was no peace. No fucking peace. He lit a cigarette, staring at the lighter shaking in his hand. Or rather his hand shaking. Screw it. He strode out of his office. Maybe a drive would help. Grab a couple of beers, something for dinner. He couldn't stand being behind that desk anymore. He was edgy. A cobra waiting to strike but denied the satisfaction.

Joe fumbled for the keys in his pocket as he approached his truck. "What the hell?" The passenger side bumper had been pushed in. Laying a hand on the hood, he bent over to inspect the damage more closely. "Son of a bitch!" He touched it and recoiled. There was blood. Just a little, but enough. Enough to know it was blood. And fur. Fur. It goddamned better be fur. His mind was spinning now, eyes flitting back and forth. Where had he been? How could he not remember hitting…something? From the size of the dent, it had to have been either a big dog or a deer. Had to be.

He ground his cigarette into the asphalt, climbed into the truck and ran his hands through his hair. There was no calming down, no relaxing. His hand was trembling as he put the key into the ignition. There was a chance. There was still a chance that this was all in his head. Maybe the concussion had done more than they thought. Shook something up. Maybe all this shit with Black was his own sick imagination. He grasped at that last straw like a drowning man clawing his way over the side of a row boat. Maybe it'd hold him… or maybe the water would win.

He turned the key. The truck's engine struggled to come to life before sputtering out. Confused, Joe tried again, knowing too well the familiar click click click that had replaced the engine sound. It wasn't even trying to start; his battery was dead. He wouldn't be going anywhere for a while. He retrieved his charger from the store room, hooked up the battery, and went inside.

The Ouija board sat pushed to the side of his kitchen table. Unused. He didn't need to touch it to know when Black was around. Black never left. He was an omnipresent anchor and Joe was going down for the third time. He supposed it could be a malignancy eating at his brain, rotting holes in his thoughts. That would even be preferable to what he thought to his core was actually happening.

He opened the bottle. Whiskey. He hated whiskey but beer didn't do it anymore. At least some bourbon would knock him out for a while and maybe when he woke the voice inside his head would be gone. He poured half a glass and stared. The cool amber liquid called to his mind and it burned as he choked it down. Another glass, another grimace. He'd taken to keeping a bottle in the house for nights like these…when he could feel the thing inside him, stretching and getting ready for…what? He didn't know. He didn't want to be conscious and he didn't want to dream.

The bottle fell. He tried to set it back up again but it kept tipping over with an empty clink. Long, deep breaths kept a rhythm in his head, so loud it seemed the air around him swelled with every exhale. The walls expanded and retreated in sync with his chest. He couldn't be dreaming; he was still at the table. But, damn. Sleep had taken him yet again, and he was in the murky darkness alone. Black would be here somewhere, cueing up some torment to push him over the cliff into insanity. He needed to find a way to wake up. If he knew he was dreaming, he could control it, right? That's what everyone said.

"Come on, Joe. You can do this," he said. "Wake up." He rubbed his hands along his thighs, then balled his right into a fist and punched himself in the leg. A charley horse knotted and he winced. A chuckle began behind him. A low baritone of dark humor.

"Fuck you." He got up from the chair and went to his silverware drawer. Everything was in disarray, but, hell, why shouldn't it be? He had no woman in his life, no stability. No control. Black had seen to that. Joe pulled out a steak knife. "It's just a dream, right? Just have to shock myself awake. Only hurts for a second, right?" He pulled the knife across his palm, slicing into his flesh. He dropped in pain, blood welling up quickly and dripping onto the kitchen tile. Nothing. No panting emergence from a nightmare, no lying in his bed sweating as checked his hand…and no relief. He pulled down a wad of paper towels and wrapped them around his bloody hand.

The chuckle had grown into laughter. "You are not in control here," he managed to spit out through clenched teeth. The creaking of rusty door hinges took his attention from his throbbing hand. He gripped the bloody paper towel more tightly and walked into the living room. His eyes darted around, looking for shadows, for something to jump out at him. Anything out of the ordinary. It was an eerie calm. He tried the side door. Locked. Well, that was good. Then the low-grade anxiety began. Locked meant things couldn't get in…but what if he couldn't get out? His mind started spinning and he needed to get ahold of himself if he was going to make it through this stinking nightmare.

A clang in the darkness. Metal across a cement floor, a hollow screech echoing through the basement. He strode to his office door and swung it open. A cold, damp air escaped past him and he peered into the room. He reached for the light switch, hit it, and of course no light came on. "Fucking typical, Mr. Black. Fucking parlor tricks." He stepped through the doorway.

It was no longer his office. Nothing was the same. In the middle of the room was a metal table. Counters lined the side walls, cabinets above them. Where was he? He ran his fingers along the cool metal table. What the hell? Another door was at the far end with an oddly shaped handle. He was shocked at how much colder it was than the rest of the room. He swung the handle down and pulled. A blast of cold air escaped and another metal table greeted him. But this one had… a duffle bag across it? He searched for a light switch. Finding one, he flipped it and immediately recoiled. It was an autopsy table and the duffel bag was a…body. Embalming table. Morgue.

"Why'd you bring me here, you sick fuck? Run out of tricks? Trying to scare me with stinking zombies now?" He paused, disgusted. He took a step closer to the body. The guy looked beaten, bloody and bruised. Practically beyond recognition. He averted his eyes from the body to the gold ring on the guy's swollen hand.

Joe stood there for what could've been minutes, or hours, when it clicked. The guy, the body, on the table. He knew who it was. The shock made him step back, hitting the wall; the cold seeping quickly into his bones. "Holy hell," he said. It was Barnes. Jack Barnes. The guy who had been so brutally murdered a few years ago. He'd read about it in the paper. The man on the rap for it said that a demon killed Barnes.

The reality of it all hit him like a ton of bricks. He scrambled to get out of the cadaver room, leaving the body and some of his sanity behind. The amusement of the thing that had brought him here was palpable. Its laughter was now a roar and the walls started closing in around him. Sliding closer, ready to choke the life out of him. Terror exploded through his nervous system. He ran, pushing through doors, and slammed into the morgue table. It knocked the wind out of him. Darkness swirled behind his eyes and he welcomed the blackout that was coming.

It was then that something grabbed him from behind and pulled him onto the table. He struggled, flailing from side to side but was pinned down. He lay there, eyes wide, breathing hard and waiting. A quiet rolling sound, as if a cart with metal wheels was approaching. Again, the tortuous wait until a motor kicked on in the darkness. Shit! He was not going to let himself be embalmed in his fucking nightmares! His heart pumped harder and faster than it ever had in his life, and he fought to get away. At the last moment, something, whatever it was, let go and he fell off the table in a full run, barely able to stand on his feet. Doors slammed and clanged in the darkness behind him, not sure where he was going or if he'd ever get back. Terror drove him. He burst through the doorway into his living room, running out the side door and up the stairs into the main entryway to Forest View. His chest heaved in pain and his lungs burned with every gasping breath. The main doors were closed, night alarm locked, and he pushed through, not caring if he triggered the alarms. He ran as if leading a stampede of demons at his heels.

Rain poured and lightning flashed. Joe collapsed about twenty feet from the building. Blackness moved through his mind, behind his eyes, and he waited for his heart to explode as he let go of his grip on consciousness.

It didn't last long. Lucidity came. Slowly at first, with that foggy confusion when you wake up in the middle of the night in an unfamiliar room. What's real; what's not? Face down, bits of broken asphalt under his cheek. His shirt clung to his chest and he realized he had been lying in the parking lot. It all came to him. Flooded back. He pushed off the ground to stand and pain ripped through his palm. Son of a bitch! He clenched his hand to his chest and when the throbbing eased, he examined it. It was blood smeared and he could make out the darker red cut across the palm. He couldn't make any sense of it. Reality mixed with nightmare mixed with… Staring at Forest View, he didn't know what to do but pick up his sorry ass and walk back inside; back to his little apartment and whatever shit might by lying in wait for him. There were no options anymore. He'd need to wrap his hand and maybe never sleep again. Shoving the main doors open, he hit the switch to silence the alarms, leaving a bloody palm print on the wall. No one would be coming. They never did anymore. He sighed, knowing what wasn't waiting for him inside was forever traveling with him in his mind. If it truly was his anymore.

Joe grabbed the laptop off his desk and brought it into the kitchen. He shoved the Ouija board to the side and sat down. An open beer, warm and half gone, was sitting on the counter. He reached for it. Swigged it. Fuck, it was awful. He took another mouthful while he waited for the home screen to load. Old and slow. Not that he could afford anything new. State of the art and cutting edge would never be a part of his life. His leg bounced nervously. He had to figure this out.

"Come on, come on," he said. Antsy. He was done with this shit. Had to find out if he was going crazy… if his brain was disintegrating into a skull of mush. *Can concussion cause hallucinations* he typed into the search bar. Should've done this before. What the hell was wrong with him? His hands were shaking, but they always seemed to have a tremor lately. Beer didn't even calm it.

Results came up on his screen. Concussion. Traumatic brain injury. Hallucinations. "Fucking A," he said as he pulled up the first article. "I knew it." There in front of him it said what he'd been looking for. There was no fucking Black, no fucking Ouija board ghost shit. It was all remnants of hitting his head on that damned rock. Confusion. Memory loss. Hallucinations. Migraines. It was all there in black and white.

He sat back in his chair, satisfied. Happy for the first time in weeks, blinking back tears; his anxiety miraculously gone. "Did you see this, Black, you fucker?" he said. "You're not fucking real. You're all in my head." He could see a doctor, heal. Get rid of this anchor around his neck. God, he could be free again.

Cool air swirled around him and goose bumps sprang up on his arms. He closed his eyes. "All in my head," he said, trying to keep the knot from tying in his stomach. "All in my fucking head." He got up, walking to the fridge for a cold one. Pulling the door open, he said, "You're not fucking real." The refrigerator door slammed shut. Joe stared at the door, then reached for the handle again. A piercing cold hand gripped his shoulder. It took everything he had to hold off the nervous tension growing inside him. "You're a figment from my fucking brain injury. Go to hell, Black. You only exist IN MY HEAD."

The hand on his shoulder whipped him around and, as he hit the wall, he saw what threw him. The shadow had to be seven feet tall. Massive. And cold. So cold. His back hit the wall with force three men couldn't have mustered and his head nailed the counter as he fell. Pain exploded through his cheek, radiating into his brain in a searing pulse. With his jaw clenched, he spit the words, "Not…fucking…real." Joe fought to hold on to consciousness, but the kitchen melted and he just let go.

13

While the boys dug through the cooler for something to eat, Amanda walked outside for a few minutes. She wanted to see if Caesar was hanging around and needed to get herself grounded once more. The residual energy in the house was a weight that kept piling in on her, slowly building on her chest until she couldn't breathe. As soon as she went down the side steps of the house, the mood eased. The large rock in the back yard seemed inviting, and she hoped Caesar would think so, too. She sat down. It was shady and cool at the edge of the woods. She closed her eyes and inhaled.

A twig snapped. She sat still, hoping the cat was as curious as everyone said cats were, and that its bravery was intact. Another twig. A small smile came to her lips. She was excited to meet this kitty. She opened her eyes and waited. Instead of the cat, she sensed a person watching her. She turned cautiously and stared into the woods, unsure of what she would see. A wisp of a small girl, a trick of her eyes? She knew better. She had grown up with these… gifts? Sensitivities? For her, it was normal. Natural. It took a long time for her to understand that other people didn't feel or see the things that she did. She peered into the woods. A barely perceptible shift of energy and it was gone. A meow from about three feet away snapped her back to her original mission.

"Well, hello, Cees," she said. "How are you, kitty cat?" She didn't move, letting Caesar decide if she was safe. "Ball's in your court." The dark gray cat paused, sizing her up. Approaching slowly, he sat down by her feet, sniffing.

"Good boy, Cees," she told him. He rubbed a chin on her shoe, keeping his eyes on her. He strolled along her leg to her hand resting on her lap. A sniff, a rub. She took all her cues from him. "There's a good kitty." She began to rub his ears, his head. A purr erupted from his chest as he leaned into her.

"Poor baby." Amanda wanted to scoop him up, bring him inside the house with her, but knew he'd bolt. He'd been afraid and on his own too long to be ready for that. Still… Caesar put a foot on her thigh, purring and rubbing, as if she were his long lost friend.

The screen door opened and closed with a slam and Brian yelled, "Ammie!"

Caesar jumped, digging a claw into Amanda's thigh as he sprung for the trees.

"Geez, Bri!" she gave him an exasperated look.

He gave her an "I'm sorry" shrug, holding out a sandwich in apology. She brushed off her pants knowing she probably had a bloody scratch forming. Caesar had bounded away, no longer able to be seen. She was sure he could still see them, though. She walked back to the house, taking the sandwich from her brother.

"Pretty cat," he offered.

She nodded, walking past him into the kitchen of 11 Ridley. Brian and Dom had already eaten and cleaned up. Damn, like a pack of wolves, she thought. Only drinks were left on the table with the equipment. "Glad you saved me a sandwich," she joked.

"We'd never forget you!" Brian said dramatically.

She ate while the guys waited. "Where do you want to start?"

"Any suggestions?" Dom asked. Many times Amanda could give them ideas, kind of guide them if she sensed anything around. Spirits had a knack for finding her. He didn't know why, but when she told them to focus in particular areas, or not, she was pretty dead on.

She shook her head. "The kitchen is the worst, but that's fairly obvious. I'm not pulling in anything more than that. Here and there a feeling, really slight. I'm almost getting more from the woods out back." She took another bite.

"What's there?"

"Not sure, exactly. I don't think it's connected to the house but when we drove up, I thought I saw the figure of a little girl. When I was out with the cat a few minutes ago, I caught a sense of her again."

"Did you make note of it?"

She nodded. "Of course," with a slight grin. Dom knew her all too well. Her "these unusual things happened to me" journal had to be about 200 pages by now. Someday maybe she'd write a book about it all. Or publish the thing on its own. Maybe. That stuff was personal. Hard to share when it hits you so deeply. It's what made the paranormal her passion. She was driven.

"I'd say, let's start from the basement. I want to do the kitchen later tonight. See if the energy in the place changes."

Amanda agreed.

"Really?" Brian was only half complaining. He loved investigating, but he hated cobwebby basements. He scooped up a voice recorder and EMF detector. "Unless you want the KII instead?" He looked at Dom.

"Might as well bring 'em both."

"I'll stay here and monitor the cameras." It hadn't needed stating. Amanda was one for details. She didn't mind hanging back. Someone had to watch the feeds and let them know if anything was going on anywhere else in the house.

Dom and Brian walked into the kitchen. "After you," Dom said, holding the basement door open.

Brian grinned at him. "Thanks a lot, Bro. Ammie! If I don't come back, you know why."

Amanda watched them on the first feed. Dom sat on the bottom step, his back to the camera. Brian was out of sight, probably sitting on the washing machine. It was just who he was. She put on the headphones and clicked the sound on the monitor so she could listen to the EVP session.

Dom and Brian alternated questions, pausing to leave time for responses in between.

"Is there anyone with us tonight who would like to make his presence known?"

"What is your name?"

"Jack, are you here with us?"

"We know you were murdered, Jack. Who did it?"

"Did you bring something back with you from your investigation at New Castle?"

"Did you use the Ouija board?"

Amanda kept her eyes on the video feeds while she listened. Sitting at base camp was never the most exciting thing to do, especially on long nights with no activity, but it was necessary. Some nights it could be as boring as watching paint dry. She laughed to herself. Hours of a camera pointed into an empty room, waiting for something to move. For a shadow to pass by. What Jack had picked up at New Castle was amazing. Well, that probably wasn't the best description. It was amazing wrapped in horrifying. Watching the video of Barnes getting attacked…like a horror movie in slow motion. Real life horror. She shook her head, trying to rid herself of the thought.

After about half an hour, Dom and Brian came strolling upstairs. "Uber quiet down there, Ammie," Brian said. "Or so it seems."

"Nothing on the cameras that I've seen, yet."

Dom nodded. "Brian, you take base camp. I want Amanda with me on the kitchen session."

Amanda gave up her seat to her brother and followed Dom into the kitchen. Her eyes darted around, almost expecting something to materialize from the residual energy that was thick around her.

"You okay?"

She gave another quick glance around and sat on a counter, her back to the cupboards. "Yeah."

Dom walked over next to her, turning the voice recorder on. He hit record. "Dom and Amanda, kitchen area, 11 Ridley, 9:30 p.m."

The kitchen was dark. Not even street lights came down this far. Regardless, Amanda closed her eyes and slowed her breathing. "Was bad here," she said. "I know, we all know that. But Barnes…he was trying to get away. It wouldn't let him." She shivered.

"The same thing that attacked him at New Castle, I'm assuming?"

"It'd have to be, from the evidence we've seen. All I feel is a… darkness. Hard to describe. The energy here is sick."

Dom nodded. He glanced around the kitchen; his eyes already adjusted to the dimness of the room. "Is there anyone here with us tonight?" He and Amanda let the seconds tick by, hopefully giving any spirit willing the time needed to absorb enough energy to be heard on the recorder. "What is your name?"

"Jack," Amanda said. "Are you here?"

"Were you murdered here?"

"Did you kill Jack Barnes?"

"Did you come from New Castle?"

"Are you attached to something here?"

Dom touched Amanda's hand. "Look outside."

She turned to see out the window over the sink toward the carport. There, sitting on the hood of her car, was Caesar. She smiled. "Poor cat. I wonder how he survived what happened here." She thought for a minute and changed her line of questioning. "Are you attached to this property?" Pause. "I've seen you standing outside. You came pretty close to me, and that's okay. You had on a very nice dress. My name's Amanda. What's yours?"

"What year is it?"

"Did you live in this house?"

"Do you know what happened here?"

"Dom, if you don't mind, I'd like to take this session outside. See if she's still hanging around out there."

"Not at all. Let's go." He called to Brian, "We're headed outside for a bit. Going to try for some EVP's."

"Not a problem. Take a hand-held with you."

Dom stopped at base camp and grabbed a small video camera, then went out into the carport with Amanda. Caesar jumped off the car but didn't run away.

"Hey, Cees, sweet kitty." She bent down, holding out her hand. Dom stood stock-still. The Russian blue sauntered to Amanda and rubbed on her leg. She gave him a couple of long body strokes, then walked to the back yard, sitting on the rock from earlier. Caesar trotted along with her, keeping an eye on Dom.

"We still recording?" she asked.

"Always."

"Are you here with us? I saw you earlier, in your pretty dress. What's your name?" She paused, trying to see if she could sense anything around them. Sometimes, things she could sense overwhelmed her. Others, everything seemed to go quiet. Dead quiet.

"This is my friend Dom. He's holding a device. If you speak next to it, we'll be able to play back the sound later and know what you said. It's our way of communicating with you."

"Hi," Dom added. He sat beside Amanda on the rock. "We're here to talk to you. To find out about you. Hear what you have to say. No one will hurt you here. We're all friends." The video camera dinged as it came on. He panned around the area, paying attention to the house and then the forest behind them.

"Dom also has a video camera. It takes moving pictures. If you are able to come closer to us, we might be able to take a video of you. Be able to see you later, when we look through it."

"That would be amazing. It'd document that you are here," Dom said.

"I'd love to know your name. Then, if I get a chance to come back and visit, we can talk again."

They waited, enjoying the summer night air.

"Can you tell me what year it is?"

"Do you like Caesar? The cat?" Amanda's questions always seemed a little more personal than Dom's. He was for getting the provable facts; she craved the communication. On any level.

"We came here to find out about what happened in this house. Do you know what happened here?"

For a split second, Amanda thought she might have seen, or sensed, a form close to the edge of the trees and motioned toward it. Dom panned in that direction, stopping where she had indicated.

"Sweetie, is that you? You can come closer to us. I promise, it's safe." Her senses seemed to be off at the moment. Maybe the residual energy in the kitchen had skewed her feelings. She took a deep breath and tried to center herself a little more.

They waited.

"Is there anything you'd like to tell us? Anything you'd like to say before we go back inside?" Amanda paused, then stood and stretched. "Thank you. It was nice visiting with you."

"Was she there?"

"Not sure. I hope so."

Caesar walked with them toward the house, but when Amanda opened the side door to go inside, he bolted under her car.

14

He waited in his truck in the Urgent Care parking lot listening to the rain fall. It had been pouring since early that morning when he came to on his kitchen floor. Thunder rumbled in the distance. He gripped the rear-view mirror, turning it so he could see his face, grimacing as pain radiated from his sore hand. Fuck all, what would have made him do that? He concentrated on his face, examining his cheek up close, until the stinging ache in his palm subsided.

His cheek, hell, his entire eye socket, was a deepening purple. Dark as an eggplant and when he touched it he saw stars. Swollen, too. He touched it again and winced. Like a kid poking a dead animal with a stick, he had to do it one more time. He was procrastinating. Putting off the inevitable…but he had to find out if anything was broken; had to see if he was going crazy. If cracking his skull on the rock had goofed up his synapses…if a tumor was eating his brain. None of his options were desirable but all were better than the one he was avoiding.

"Fill out this form and someone will be right with you," the receptionist said. Forms, always the damned forms. You'd think he'd be in their computer system already. Check this, check that. Has your address changed since the last time you fucked yourself up? Do you have insurance or are we whisking you out the revolving door? Yeah, he didn't like this place or its forms. Staring at the paper made his head hurt, and when he looked down the throbbing in his cheek stabbed him like a steady, pulsing ice pick. He signed his name and

153

handed it to another woman behind a glass window. *Co-payments expected at the time of visit. No exceptions.* Had he even brought his wallet? He felt his back pocket and sighed. At least he hadn't lost all his faculties. Yet. He sat down in one of the stiff waiting room chairs.

By the time they called his name, he had already finished one news show and started another. The TV was mounted in the corner of the room, high up on the wall. He guessed that way kids didn't put their dirty fingers on the screen and no one tried changing the channels. For being Urgent Care, there wasn't much urgency here. More like Monotonous Care. He followed the nurse down a short hallway and into a small examination room. Three walls and privacy was a curtain away. She was pretty cute, too, if someone could be cute in shapeless scrubs. For a quick moment, he wondered how much it would take to get her on the table with him.

"So, Mr. Paine, what brings you here today?"

Of all the goddamned stupid questions to ask. Could she not see his face? Read the papers he had filled out? He would've rolled his eyes if it didn't hurt like a son of a bitch.

"My face," he said.

"Yes. How'd it happen?" She pulled on some latex gloves and lightly pressed on the skin around his cheekbone, then unslung her stethoscope and moved on to his vitals.

"I fell. In my kitchen. Guess I hit my head on the counter."

"Did you lose consciousness?"

"Um, yeah."

"Any idea how long?"

"No, not really."

"Minutes? Hours?"

"I don't know. I woke up on the floor."

She took his temperature, clicking the plastic cover into the trash. "98.6."

Not that he had half a clue as to why that would be relevant. At least she didn't ask him to stand on the scales. You're here for a broken leg? Can you hop this way for me? He would have raised an eyebrow at her if he could have without blacking out.

"Okay, well, the doctor will be in shortly. I'm sure he's going to want to send you for x-rays, make sure nothing is broken."

Joe nodded. "Yeah, I figured. I'd also like to talk to him about a few other things going on."

"I'll let him know," she was already pulling off her gloves and on her way out of the room.

Yup. Move you in, move on, move you out. God, he hoped the doctor didn't take long. Sitting in the exam room amped up his anxiety.

After about half an hour the doctor finally showed, with a starched white jacket attitude. He sauntered in like he owned the place, pushing one of those little carts with a laptop. They all did that now. Why look a man in the eye when you can stare into a little screen, checking his insurance instead of his symptoms? The doc did the perfunctory check, yes, yes, hmm. Definitely need an x-ray, maybe broken, will have to see. Yadda, yadda, will be back after they get the pictures of your face. Three minutes and the guy was out the door. Well, curtain.

Another wait. His annoyance grew with every tick of the clock and ache of his cheek. The x-ray had been quick. The technician was a friendly, older woman who was obviously tired of taking pictures of body parts day in and day out. Uninterested. Sit this way, turn that. Move this, if it doesn't hurt too much…wham, bam, and he was back sitting in the original exam room on the same stinking plastic table with the crunchy paper.

He laid down. Every time he caught the nurse's attention, she gave him that imbecilic, sympathetic grin and shrug. The "oh, I know it's taking a long time, if I could change it, I would" bullshit. He wondered how many people blew through there each day and got that same face. "It'll freeze that way," his mother used to say. He hoped so. Would serve her right. He went to rub his eyes without thinking and recoiled as he hit his swollen flesh. Damn, this day was dragging. You'd think they would have given him a Tylenol. Something!

The doctor returned and showed Joe the x-rays.

"Nothing is broken. You're very lucky. Just quite a bruise. I can give you something for the pain, or Tylenol is good, too. Ice packs. It should ease up in a few days. Take a couple weeks to be gone completely." He was halfway out the "door" before Joe could stop him.

"Wait, Doc. I have some questions."

The doctor turned, almost annoyed. Sheesh. It wasn't as if there were thirty heart attacks or a fifty-car pileup with multiple ambulances at the door. Two of the three other urgent rooms were empty.

"Yes?"

"I was wondering…I had a concussion a few weeks ago. I'm having some odd symptoms that I was thinking were related."

"Like what? What symptoms?"

"Headaches. Dizziness…and…"

"And?"

"Seeing things that shouldn't be there. Hearing things. I don't know if it's hallucinations or what. Physical things."

The doctor made a few notes. "Those things can all happen from a traumatic brain injury, sure, sure. But, I'm only the doctor on call. You need to follow up with your primary physician."

"I don't have one. Only the doctor I saw in the emergency room when it happened."

"Ah, okay," he stared down at his laptop.

Joe wanted to tell him, "My eyes are up here," like when men stared too long at a girl's tits, but figured the guy would blow him off if he did. Or send him to some crackpot who'd say he needed to be institutionalized or some shit. He bit his tongue.

"I can refer you to a neurologist. The girls at the desk can give you his number."

"Is there someone I can see today? I need to get this figured out."

"I don't think that would be…"

Joe cut him off. "Please, Doc. I think that's why this," he pointed at his cheek, "happened. I'm… worried." His voice had more than an air of desperation. "Please."

The doctor studied him for a moment, taking it all in. "Let me see what I can do." He disappeared from view and Joe could hear his voice from a little farther down the hall.

"Here," the doctor said when he returned. He pressed a piece of paper into Joe's hand. "Go to the third floor, suite 302. Dr. Reynolds. He makes his rounds today but said he'd try to fit you in. He'll talk to you in his office and take it from there."

Relief flooded him. "Thanks, Doc. Thanks a lot." He shook the Urgent Care doctor's hand and left to find the third floor.

Joe opened the door to his truck and threw the paperwork inside. Scripts for an MRI, a psychiatric evaluation, blood tests! Test after fucking test, blah blah blah. He was pissed off enough he flew like a tornado past the receptionist on his way out. Bill him for the shitting copays. He didn't care. *A mild concussion such as yours should not be causing the effects you're describing, Mr. Paine. Do you use drugs or alcohol? Have you ever been diagnosed with any type of mental disorder?*

He had tried to explain how everything started after the blow to the head, but the doc only wanted to concentrate on his past. He answered the questions as best he could, yes, he drank alcohol. No, no drugs. He didn't mention that he used to smoke weed but he hardly thought that mattered. It'd been a few years, anyway. Since his dealer went to jail. Hah. So much for that. Maybe some weed would be helpful. Question after question, leading to nowhere. He was entirely pissed. He got it, he got it. The tests would rule out other things but he felt scrutinized. Judged. Like there must be something inherently wrong with him and that it wasn't from his accident. Maybe he should have brought up the Ouija board and Black. HAH. He'd be sitting in the looney bin if he had. Locked away.

Well, we can't let that happen, can we?

Joe's stomach twisted into a knot at the sound of Black's voice. He tried to ignore it as goosebumps rippled across his skin and the temperature in the truck dropped. Absently, he hit the off button on the air conditioner, even though he knew it wasn't on. He shifted into reverse, determined to back out of his parking space and leave this feeling behind but now he could see his breath. The window fogged over. He was breathing hard, stunned that his front window was covered in frost. Joe stuck out his arm, placing his palm flat against the window. The ice melted at his touch, drips running down his wrist to his elbow, then drip drip dropping to his seat. It had to be 85 degrees outside and, yet, in his truck it was below 32.

Do you really believe I'm your imagination, Joe?

He leaned back against the driver's seat, eyes shut. Trying to control the tremor going through his body.

DO YOU?

Without opening his eyes, Joe could barely whisper, "No."
Black's laughter shook him from the inside out, more than his trembling ever could have. It erupted from within and around him, then was gone. A pause. An emptiness. When he opened his eyes, the windshield had melted clear and was a sea of condensation. He swiped at it with an old shirt on the seat beside him, then wiped his eyes with it, as well. He drove home and sat in his truck for an hour

or two, knowing it was meaningless where he was or what he did anymore, but not ready to head into his tomb. He wouldn't be keeping the appointments the doc had made. Black had other plans.

15

"Hey, Bri," Amanda called, letting the screen door bang shut. "We're back." They milled around base camp for a few minutes, uploading from the voice recorder to the computer. Amanda looked at Dom. "What's the plan?"

"We've got to address the living room, the reports of the kitchen door opening and closing. I think it's hang out for a while, monitor the feeds and wait. Maybe another EVP session on the basement stairs. See if anything starts walking through the attic crawlspace."

She nodded. "Feels really quiet, at this point."

The rest of the night was equally still. By the time they turned on the lights and started to break down the equipment, it was after 3:00 a.m. Brian stretched. "This was a real slow one."

"Yeah," Amanda said. "I think that we need to start planning step two, even before we hit evidence review."

Dom raised an eyebrow as he wound cable around his arm.

"New Castle or whatever place stands there now. Forest Hills, Forest View, something like that. I think that's where we need to go to figure out what the deal is."

"Definitely," Brian added. "We need to find out whatever we can about what Barnes tangled with. I mean, I don't want to tangle with it myself, but, come on. It's what we do, right?"

Dom smiled. "Yeah, it is. If you're both up for it, we can start making calls tomorrow. I want this evidence reviewed and sorted before we head over. If they'll even let us in. Just in case there's something recorded, something we may have overlooked. I want all our ducks in a row before we potentially kick up something bigger."

Immediately energized by the thought of the next investigation, Brian began taking down the cameras. "Don't forget the recorder in the crawlspace," he told Dom.

Once outside, Dom and Brian had the van packed quickly. Amanda stood beside her car, staring off into the distance.

"Communicating with the great beyond, Sis?"

"Huh? Oh, nah. Just watching him," she pointed to Cees, off in the distance. "Do you think he'd come with me?"

"You're thinking of taking the cat?" Brian asked. "Really?"

"He doesn't have a home. Lost and alone, and who knows if we'll get back here again for me to try? Especially if the house gets sold."

Dom paused before slamming the van doors shut. "Forever the rescuer of little lost souls," he said.

She smiled at him.

"Go ahead. I don't think Brian and I can help. We'll wait while you try." Dom leaned against the van.

Amanda walked to the edge of the carport and sat on the asphalt. "Come on, Cees. Trust me, baby. I won't hurt you." She held out her hand, hoping he'd at least get close enough to sniff her fingers. She waited. Eventually, and ever so slowly, Ceasar approached. One eye on Dom and the van, one on the sweet girl he had befriended. He rubbed against her hand. He tentatively stepped onto her lap and settled against her, purring as if his life depended on it. Safe.

Amanda pet him and cooed, hugging him close. She hesitated before wrapping one arm around him and standing up, caressing under his neck at the same time. He stiffened as if he wanted to see if she was going to take him inside. The house was non-negotiable. But she knew that. She tried to not even misstep in that direction.

"Okay, Boys," she said quietly. "Let's see what happens when I get in the car."

It wasn't the easiest, trying to open her car door and slide in with

Caesar, but Dom knew he and Brian couldn't step in. Amanda, at the very least, would become a scratching post, while the terrified feline would fly out of any opening he could find. Amanda let him settle on her lap once again, then closed the door. She turned the ignition and cracked the window, giving Dom and Brian a thumbs up. They drove home, Dom's hands on the wheel, Brian pawing through the cooler, and Amanda driving one handedly while petting her new friend and addition to the family. Cees purred and fell asleep for his most restful night in nearly 2 years.

16

0 degrees Fahrenheit. The early morning sun reflected across the frozen lake. Joe turned off his snowmobile and surveyed the area, taking a deep breath of fresh mountain air. It had snowed the night before, with a few animal tracks the only disturbance for miles. The trees across the lake could have been out of a painting. He smiled and sighed, gathering his ice fishing equipment. Every footstep crunched. He loved this time of year, with the air crisp and the ice thick.

He piled his auger, tackle box and tip-ups, stadium chair and fishing pole onto his small sport sled and dragged it onto the ice. No one else had been up to this spot in years. He kept it to himself, owning the acreage and maintaining the Posted signs. It was his sanctuary.

The perfect spot was waiting about twenty feet out. He grabbed his auger and drilled down through the ice. The water gave a little splash as he broke through, and he chiseled around the sides of the hole, working it to about six inches. Wide and ready. Another glance around the lake, soaking in its beauty, and he opened up his chair. He settled into it, tackle box at his feet and pole across his lap. This was his day and he was going to savor every minute.

He pawed through his box, searching for just the right lure, and got it set on his line. Something shifted in his peripheral vision and he looked up. What the…? He stood, letting his pole drop beside the hole. He had expected a buck or even the stray black bear, but instead there were multiple ice fishing spots across the lake. HIS LAKE. His eyes inspected the shore, looking for where these people had gained access to his land. There was nothing. No sign of entry, no snow machines, not even a frozen-over footstep. And there was no one on the lake.

He paused. At least eight other spots and no one watching them. No one fishing, no one on the shore. How did that make any sense? He stood, staring out at the ice, taking in the quiet, eerily empty atmosphere when the flag at the farthest spot flipped up. Before he could move, or ponder anything more, the next flag tipped up. Then a third. A fourth. A little faster this time, coming toward him. Anticipation changed to trepidation. He could almost feel Jaws-like music as each spot was triggered, as if something was picking up speed moving toward him. Like when the shark was harpooned and took the barrels, one after another, deep into the ocean. Everything would go disarmingly calm before chaos erupted and it attacked. His pulse picked up and he could feel his heart beating harder. Another flag turned upward, the next and, with only two flags left before whatever it was was at his hole, he decided to leave. Watch from the shore to see if anything more came of this…see what possible school of fish could be traveling like this…in a beeline for him. Some weird nature manifestation of an intelligent salmon, bent on attacking the guy with the hook. He turned, taking one step toward the land as he heard the final two flags click high.

Water rushed through the hole, ice shattered and cold, searing pain tightened around his ankle. He bent over, beating at the hand that was trying to pull him into the icy water. He scrambled, sliding along the water-slick ice, desperately clawing for a foothold and pulling at the fingers burning into his flesh. Flailing as he disappeared into the lake.

He thrashed, the black-blue water and bright sun merging into a sea of confusion. He was fighting battles for air, for life. Something had him, was pulling him deeper into the frigid water. But how was IT breathing? What had him? In desperation, he let go of whoever, whatever, had his leg and frantically pawed at the ice above him. He had to find an opening or all was over. He could no longer feel; his hands were useless clubs against ice that had been thickly frozen for weeks.

The thing around his ankle gave a final pull, dragging him along under the ice and Joe went limp. He let go knowing he was finished, knowing whatever had him was going in for the kill. He opened his mouth to inhale, to suck water into his lungs and end this horror show of a life, as he was thrust through the hole and up onto the ice beside his equipment. He lay there disbelieving and panting, pulling that crisp, cold air into his hungry lungs. Soaked to the bone and aching, half numb, he pulled himself along the ice, too terrified to try to stand and walk. He crawled to the snowmobile.

He rolled over, pulling the blanket up to his chin. Stabbing pain nailed his left ankle, like an ice pick moving in slow motion through his leg and out the other side. He threw off the covers to examine it, falling back into his pillows with a hand over his eyes. The ankle was a mix of black and dark blue, with the darkest flesh flaking off. He knew what it was, recognized it from his hiking days. Frostbite. Severe frostbite. In the shape of a hand. He didn't question how or why. He knew whose. Sobs intertwined with manic laughter took him over. He was done. Destroyed. Message received.

His work phone was ringing as he pulled his ass out of bed. The door between his office and apartment was never closed anymore. Life was a blur, if you could call it a life. He lived, worked, and existed wherever Black took him. The ringing continued. He heard it, loud and persistent, and would have let it go to voicemail but the demon in his head made that impossible. He stumbled through his living room, limping, and grabbed his dick. Rock hard and needing to pee, he guessed Black didn't worry about things like that.

"Yeah, Forest View. Office," he didn't even try to hide his frustration. Hell, it wasn't even 10:00 am yet. He didn't think he'd gotten to work before noon in the last three weeks and what the hell was so important anyway?

"Hello. Dom Giordano, from Out of the Dark Paranormal. Is there a manager I could speak to?"

"That's me. Joe Paine."

"Mr. Paine," Dom said.

Joe rubbed his temples. "Joe is fine." A dull headache had taken hold, whether from the Smirnoff's last night or the son of a bitch's nightmares, he didn't know.

"Okay, Joe. I work with a team of paranormal investigators

and…" Dom was still talking, but for Joe the words trailed off. Owners of the property, yes, yes, he was in contact with them quite often. Oh, yes, he could speak for them. Ghost hunters? Yes, very interesting.

A roaring began in his ears and he fought to keep up with what was being said. He nodded, pressing his hand into his temple and trying to keep his mind on the conversation. He hid it well; elbow on the table, leaning, pushing his head against his fingers, voice barely wavering. If he could have, he would have shoved his hand into his brain and pulled the fucker out. But he couldn't do that, now could he? Black's presence circled around him, chilling the air.

He put his phone on speaker and let his other hand ball into a fist as he talked. "Yes, yes," his head throbbed, ached with the darkness that was overtaking him. He pulled open the pencil drawer, hearing the chink of the ring he had tossed in weeks ago. "Absolutely. I understand. An interview and then a walkthrough?" He rolled it around in his hand a moment before sliding it onto his ring finger. It fit like a glove.

The guy on the other end of the phone droned on. The rush in Joe's ears grew louder. The words spiraled, confusing him. Why did this guy make his mind pulse? He had to get off the call before his skull exploded. "It…it's fine. Yeah, we can do that. Overnight?"

The voice talking at him was now nails on a blackboard. Not fingernails, but fucking coffin nails. Sealing his fate. Or someone else's. He felt his words coming out more strained, tighter. He was losing control.

"Saturday? The second?" He didn't look at his calendar, wouldn't have seen it if he tried. Migraine times a thousand, filled with vile thoughts. "Yeah. 2 p.m. Sure. See you then." He killed the call. It'd be lucky if that was all he killed. His eyes went dark for a moment, then cleared. It was time to clock out and head…somewhere.

By the time he was dressed, he had it figured out. Things needed fixing. Upgrading. He checked the lock on his office door and found it lacking. It would be fine for any old office door, but his was more important. The storage room door at the end of the hallway was also embarrassingly behind the times, security-wise. The wire mesh walls seemed pretty secure, but he definitely had to change up that lock. How the hell did the contractors miss that? He'd take care of it, though. He'd have everything ready and installed before those ghost hunters came. It was necessary to have everything in top shape when they arrived. Joe left Forest View with a plan.

He picked up the brown paper bags and nodded a curt thank you at the clerk. The sunglasses hid the anger in his eyes. Shoving the glass door open triggered the bell above it. The double ding pierced his brain and the sunshine made him squint in spite of the darkness of his lenses. Most of the time now he felt like Stephen King's Cujo. If only. If only he were rabid. He'd gladly run head first into the side of a car until his brains spilled down the side. At least then the headaches would stop. And the blackouts. And the…

"Great. Just fucking great," he said. Up ahead, between him and his truck, was a sea of senior citizens. It was their monthly trip to Freemont, this time to the county historical museum on Main Street. As he got closer he heard one old woman say, "Funny how they take old relics to see older relics." Her companions all laughed and agreed.

"Come on, come on," he weaved through the crowd, all moving toward the large blue bus parked at the curb. He bumped into one of the women and she turned, touching his arm.

"I'm sorry. I didn't mean to be in your…" She looked into his face. He stared, expressionless behind his sunglasses. She let go of his arm and took a step back, absently wiping her hand on her sweater. The rest of her friends continued on toward the bus, moving around her like a stream pours around a rock. "I… I…" was all she could get out. She had come up against this wrongness before. She had felt this…before. "I know you."

Joe smirked. "You knew Jack."

The color drained from her face. "Mabel, come on! Better come along or we'll leave without you," one of the other women called. Hands shaking, Mabel adjusted her hat and turned toward the bus. She steeled herself against his gaze and walked away, trying not to look back.

"Mabel! What's wrong?" There were some shouts and confusion. A woman yelled for help, for someone to call 911. Mabel laid on the sidewalk, her right hand balled into a fist on her chest. Someone picked up her large fern-green hat from the sidewalk and fanned her with it.

"Could it be her heart?"

"She never had a heart problem."

"Oh, please let her be okay."

As a small crowd gathered where Mabel had collapsed, Joe's sneer widened. He had more work to do. He climbed into his truck while sirens sounded in the distance.

17

Amanda pulled Vinnie into the Forest View parking lot and parked next to Dom's van. She gazed at the newly constructed apartment complex, looking for some tell-tale sign of a dark resident. It all seemed friendly enough, clean and landscaped. She could envision happy families on their balconies, maybe a new swing set or climbing gym off to the side. Eventually. Picture perfect. She shivered. 80 degrees out and she had goosebumps. Dom opened his door and got out, while Brian, eating a Big Mac, leaned over to see her.

"Hey, Sis," he said between bites.

She gave him a quick wave and turned to Dom. "Creepy place."

"Is it?"

She nodded. "A bit."

Dom surveyed it. To him, it was just a building with an intriguing history and the potential of a haunting. "Bad?"

Amanda shrugged. "We'll see," she paused. "Did you get to review any of the footage from the other night? The audio?"

"Yeah. Nothing in the house, but we did get a little something when we were outside. Here," he shuffled around in his pocket for his phone. "I have the clip here."

He played it for Amanda.

We came here to find out about what happened in this house. Do you know what happened here?

171

Faintly, the slightest childlike whisper came across.

Yesss.

Amanda's eyes got wide. "She's there! I knew it. I knew I felt her."

Dom smiled, and waited.

"Oh, my God. She knows what happened there." She locked eyes with Dom. "We have to go back. I want to talk to her."

"I knew you'd say that."

"Can we? Do you think we can get permission?"

"That, I don't know. We can try."

The passenger door slammed shut. He had his still camera dangling off his wrist. "Are we ready to go in or what?"

"We've still got a few minutes."

"Great, I wanted some outside shots," his words were almost lost as he had already turned and was jogging closer to the complex. "I'm going to try to get the angles Barnes got."

"I know," Dom said. He expected nothing less. "The manager said he'd meet us at the front doors at 2:00 p.m.."

Joe was already in the lobby when they started walking toward the building. He'd been waiting out of sight for the last twenty minutes, keeping an eye for them. An interview. Should be easy enough. A tour of the place. His place. Walkthrough, they called it. Intruding, he called it. He sized them up as they got to the doorway.

Holding out his hand, he greeted them with his biggest, overly sincere smile. "Paine. Joe Paine. You must be Out of the Dark?"

Dom shook his hand. "Yes. I'm Dom and this is Brian and Amanda."

"Come in, come in," he ushered them into the lobby. "And, please, call me Joe. Oh, and forgive the sunglasses. I was at the eye doctor and he dilated my eyes. A real pain in the neck."

A blast of cool, air-conditioned air met them as they stood in the entrance to Forest View. It was relatively peaceful, with muted tones of yellow and beige in the wallpaper flowers, a few overstuffed chairs arranged pleasantly. Amanda shivered.

"So, tell me…what's first?" Joe asked. "You mentioned an interview?"

"Yes," Dom said. "We'd like to sit down with you for a few minutes and ask you some questions about this place. It's history, your history here, things like that. It may help fill in some gaps in our research."

"Well, as much as I like the lobby, we'll be more comfortable in my office. It's this way."

They walked downstairs, Amanda paused to get her bearings. She pushed off the feeling of dread that started to claw at her as they stopped in front of Joe's office door. He unlocked it and they went in. "I keep the office locked. Good practice." As Amanda crossed the threshold, she ran her fingers along the doorframe.

They settled into the chairs he had arranged around his desk. He took his seat in a high backed black leather chair. "What would you like to know?"

Amanda brought out her clipboard. She began with the usual questionnaire they used for this process. How long have you lived here, worked here? How long has the building been on the property? The history of the building, dates renovated. Have you noticed any activity that couldn't be explained?

"Well, I'm sure you know the history of New Castle…all that takes is a little poking around the internet. Obviously plenty of other people have found out. Before they tore the old place down, there were teenagers here trying to summon 'the dark lord,' or some shit, if you'll excuse my language. People trespassing where they shouldn't. I don't get the attraction to old abandoned buildings. Or ghosts, for that matter. I've never had a paranormal experience in my life, let alone anything happen here," Joe said.

"No odd noises, no objects out of place, nothing?"

"Nope. I sleep soundly and have always been completely comfortable here. Sorry to disappoint."

"Oh, not at all," Dom said. "We come in with a scientific mindset. We want to document what's here, or not, so it can add to our research and investigation from another location."

"Jack Barnes' house," Joe said. "And what did you find there?"

Brian glanced at Dom, who hesitated answering.

Joe smirked. "It's the only logical conclusion. You did an investigation, wanted to come here. Everyone knows Barnes was poking around in the asylum before he killed himself."

"Killed himself?" Brian asked. "The guy was beaten to a pulp."

"Yeah, but who knows? Some say his buddy did it, the buddy said the devil did it. I think he offed himself and his friend was in the wrong place at the wrong time."

"We would've liked to have been able to speak with him about it all, but he died recently."

"Yes, I heard. Committed suicide. Weak mind. Couldn't deal. Barnes was weak, too. Couldn't handle what life threw at him."

"And what do you think life threw at him?"

"Oh, I was speaking in general terms. No one will ever really know, will they?" Joe said. "Did you find anything…interesting at his place?"

"I can't divulge anything at this point."

Joe waved it off. "Not a problem. I totally understand confidentiality, letting the client know first, yadda yadda. I'm sure you'll treat this investigation the same."

"Yes, of course. I have forms right here for you to look over and sign. The usual releases. If we get hurt on the property, it's all on us, and so on."

Joe took the papers and gave a look through, setting them on the side of his desk. "Have we met before?" Joe asked Amanda. Dom and Brian turned to look at her.

"No, I don't think so." She fidgeted with her pencil, shifting in her chair.

"You don't like it here, do you?"

The direct questions made her uneasy and the heaviness of the room was unsettling. "I'm sorry. I need some air." She handed her clipboard to Dom. "If you'll excuse me." She could feel Joe's eyes boring into her back as she left.

"These rooms used to be part of the original morgue. Must be a bitch for her."

Brian's eyes lit up and he looked around more intently, trying to imagine the room the way it must've been. "How did you know that Ammie was psychic?"

"She was uncomfortable from the minute she walked in. Doesn't take a rocket scientist. Now, what other questions did you have before you tour this lovely place?"

Amanda took a walk around the building when she got outside. Nothing felt completely okay on the grounds. It was hard to get centered, to push away the negativity that was bombarding her. She strolled across the lawn, looking at the marigolds and petunias planted along the walkway. The little balconies were pristine and inviting. She was glad they got to investigate before anyone moved in, but no part of her was happy to be here. She expected an old asylum to have a "feel," but she never thought it would have a pulse. A heartbeat. She shivered. Maybe she was being overdramatic. Letting her mind run away with whatever she was picking up. It could all be residual. A lot of energy left over from the patients. Whatever Barnes had encountered might be long gone by now. Key word *might*. Somehow, she doubted it. And that manager. Damn. She was sure she recognized his voice.

She circled to the back of the building and wandered a little closer to the tree line. It was calmer there. Quieter, energy-wise. She stood still to ground herself, then moved closer to the woods. A few gray stones in the bushes took her attention. They were small and overgrown, nearly covered by the undergrowth. Gravestones. Nothing fancy, without even last names. Unusual. Just a handful of markers, noting those who had passed on. Probably patients from the asylum. Perhaps without even family to grieve for them. She snapped some pictures on her cell phone and jotted a few notes to herself. With a deep breath, she turned toward Forest View. It was time to push on.

Amanda joined the men as they stood to leave the office. Dom raised an eyebrow. "All good?" he asked.

She nodded, already feeling the energy of the basement trying to erode the walls she had put up.

"So glad you're back," Joe said. "We were going to start the walkthrough. I would hate for you to have missed any of it."

"Thanks. The air helped." Amanda took her clipboard from Dom, holding it against her chest with her arms crossed.

"Well, let's get started," Joe pushed away from his desk, holding his arms wide. "This wonderful little room was originally the morgue. A gruesome table probably stood about where my desk is now and the cold room was off that wall." Brian walked over and touched it, as if he could feel the chill from all those years ago. He turned on the Mel-Meter. "No time like the present," he said. He moved the meter along the wall, checking for any changes in its readout.

"Nothing unusual here. A few hits, but I'm sure it's spikes off the computer equipment and wiring." He continued around the perimeter of the room.

Joe waited as patiently as he could and then stepped toward the doorway into his apartment. He hated being amiable for these people. Black despised them, but, for some reason, wanted them here. All he could do was go along with it. "My apartment was built where a medical room stood, adjacent to the morgue. Perhaps as patients died, they were moved right onto the slab." He smirked. "Not much to see here now."

Amanda made notes and Joe ushered everyone through his office into the hallway.

"Do you know of any activity reported in the morgue area?" Dom asked. He and Brian had been chatting about where to position cameras.

"None," Joe said. "Dead quiet in there. No one has even been in here since it was renovated except for workers and myself."

"I think we need a camera," Brian said.

"Do what you will. There are more interesting parts to this building, in my opinion." He walked on to the storage room and waited for them to catch up. He laid his palm against the mesh wall. "This had been a day room for patients before the current owners came in. Kind of a common room, I guess." He swung open the door, sliding a wooden wedge in at the bottom to keep it from swinging back at them. Brian walked in, watching for any change in the meter readout. "The workers found a few old drawings on the walls before they demolished the asylum. Must've been done by patients waiting for the docs to see them. Hate that wait myself."

"All zeros," Brian said. Amanda made a quick note. If anything changed later, they'd have her notes to compare it to. She recorded everything she could throughout their investigations. It was who she was. Thorough.

As Brian walked out of the storage room, Amanda shivered. Maybe from the air conditioning or maybe from the room. She was unsure. The whole building made her uneasy. Joe kept watching her, too, which added to the creep factor. There was something about him she couldn't put her finger on.

As they checked out the lobby and started down the first-floor hallway, Brian tried one of the apartment doors. Locked. "Will we have access to the rooms during the investigation?"

Joe shook his head. "No. The owners didn't like the idea of strangers walking through the rentals." Not that he even checked with the owners. He made the decisions here. This was his place. His.

"Fair enough," Dom said. He had wanted to do a walkthrough of each one with Amanda, see what she felt and hit some of the areas where Barnes had gotten activity, but rules were rules. His reputation, and the team's, was built on respect and professionalism.

"No worries," Joe said. "You'll get to some of the more interesting places. You already probably have a pretty good idea of where Jack Barnes investigated."

"An idea, yes. I think down this hallway was the laundry room?"

"Yeah, I think so. I haven't looked at the plans in a long time, but I think it was at the very end of this hallway."

They walked along, with educated guesses at which doors belonged to the old laundry space. Dom wished they could have gotten permission to go inside, but they'd do what they could.

"Stairs?" Joe asked.

The second floor looked like the first. The usual beige carpeting and non-descript wallpaper. Amanda paused at the top of the staircase, took a breath and walked on. Joe timed his steps to match hers and it brought an edginess that bordered on unnerving; as though she was walking through a tunnel that got narrower and narrower the farther she went. What was his issue? The air felt heavier. She could picture this hallway from the video that Jack made. The chipped plaster. The graffiti. Her pace slowed.

"What do you think of this floor, Amanda?" He drew out the syllables of her name and it echoed in her mind.

"Not the friendliest place I've ever been." She made a few more notes on her yellow pad.

Dom and Brian went straight to the end, touching the walls and looking at the floor. Commenting on what the camera angle should be.

"You know, it's still there," Joe said.

Dom turned. "Excuse me?"

"It's still there." Joe pointed at the floor. "The pentagram."

Brian stared at the floor, as if sheer curiosity would make it visible.

"There was a pentagram?" Dom asked. He was in no way going to let on or give out the knowledge they already had.

Joe eyed Dom and each sized up the other. "Why, yes. There was," Joe replied. "The work of vandals."

"How could it still be there?" Brian asked. "Wasn't New Castle was razed?"

"Not entirely, no. And some things can never be erased."

"We did read through some of the local newspaper articles about New Castle. I guess it was kind of a hot spot for kids looking to have a good scare," Dom said.

"At least that."

"What?" Brian asked.

"Nothing. A lot of trespassers came through in the years the asylum was empty. Since building the apartments it's been quiet as a tomb." He smiled at Brian. "So, tell me," he folded his arms across his chest and leaned against the wall, "in your 'ghost hunting,' have you ever used a Ouija board?"

"No," Dom said.

"I mean, I know it's a kid's game, Parker Bros. and all, but people say…"

"Definitely not," Brian said. "You never know what might be coming through. You see, it's all about the intent of the person using it. Doesn't have to be a Ouija board…could be anything, if you're focused on communication with the other side. Works like a portal and anything can step through. It's dangerous. Especially in a place with a lot of negative energy."

"Have you ever used one, Joe?" Dom asked.

"Me? Oh, no. Never. Just curious, was all."

"I'd steer clear of them, that's for sure. Why mess with something you can't control?"

Joe nodded. "Why indeed."

Amanda stopped writing. "Okay, so where are we setting up base camp?"

"I'm thinking the lobby?" Brian asked. "It's central, and since no one lives here yet, we shouldn't be in anybody's way." They all turned to Joe.

"That should be fine," Joe said. "It's where Barnes set up, isn't it?"

"It may have been," Dom said. "You seem to know an awful lot about Barnes' investigation."

"Everyone kept up on the trial. It was all the town could talk about for quite a while. Satan worshippers, a ghost hunter dead. It was like our own little horror story. Barnes had been through the town himself before he came here, asking questions. Nobody was thrilled about him prying into the past. It's our history. Good or bad."

"A close-knit bunch, huh?"

"Sometimes a past can tie people together. When there's nothing else to hold onto, they always have that," Joe said. "It's their own."

"I suppose that's true," Dom said. "But what makes this place different than any other institution? They all had their taste of abuse and neglect. Why is this site special?"

Joe's eyes narrowed behind his sunglasses. "Maybe that's what you're here to find out." He paused and the air seemed to thicken. "The lobby should be fine. Do you need me to get anything for you?"

Brian shook his head. "Thanks, we're good."

Joe left them in the lobby and went downstairs into his apartment. He stopped in the kitchen for a cold one and saw that all four stove burners were on and bright red. "Shit!" he quickly whipped at the knobs, trying not to burn his fingers. He wasn't surprised. Pissed was more like it. The son of a bitch kept him on his toes, that was for sure. Seemed like there was nowhere he could relax, or even let his guard down, anymore. He grabbed a beer and held it against his forehead, wishing he could make some sense out of his life.

"Um, Joe?"

He jumped, nerves frayed. "Almost give me a heart attack." Joe grabbed the bottle opener off the counter and popped the top off his beer. He pointed it at Brian. "You need to be careful. That could be dangerous."

"Sorry. You must not have heard me yell." Brian glanced at the table. He recognized something sticking out from under a pile of mail. "Nice spirit board."

Joe stiffened, his grip tightening on the bottle. "It's not mine," he smiled. A little too wide, a little too reassuring. "Keeping it for a friend." The kid didn't need to know the friend was Black and he was no fucking friend.

"Oh. Hence your question about boards…" Brian's voice trailed off. Joe was lying, he knew it. Hell, Joe knew it.

"Yeah. So, what's up? Come looking for a beer?" He tipped the bottle toward Brian, offering him one.

"Hah. No, thanks. I was wondering if you care where we put the camera in your office? I'd like to get a wide shot of the room."

He followed Brian into the office, looking around. "No, put it wherever's best for you guys." Brian nodded standing in the center of the room. He started spying the best spot for the video camera, pausing by Joe's desk. The top right drawer was partially open and he could see the handle of a handgun.

"So," Brian said. "You find much need for protection here?"

"Excuse me?"

Brian gestured toward the drawer. "Been thinking of getting my license. What kind is it?"

"9 mm. Smith and Wesson," Joe said, shoving the drawer closed. "No one's needed it. Yet." He strode into his apartment and closed the door.

Joe sat at his kitchen table; his head aching and angry. Knowing those three "ghost hunters" were wandering around was driving him up the wall. He wanted to throw things. Break things. Feel them shattering. Black wanted them there, yet didn't want them in this space. His space. It was getting harder to separate his feelings from Black's and he lived in a frustrated confusion. There were only shreds of moments where he actually saw through his own eyes, and the things he had seen he wished he hadn't. Black controlled those moments; torturing him with glimpses of how his life was in the toilet now. There was no going back. No life to return to. He was ruined and he was taking everything he touched down with him.

A spike of pain went through his temple and he cried out. Collapsing into a fetal position, he rocked to the rhythm of the pain. There was no thought or hope. He wanted that comfort of a child in his mother's arms yet could only try to fight off Black's suffocating tendrils.

Something hit the wall. He waited for the agony to subside to a dull throb and looked up. A knife. A knife was imbedded in the wall. It could've been right out of an episode of Chopped on the cooking channel. A fucking butcher knife sticking out of his wall. Darkness churned, his vision fading. He was blacking out again and was terrified he would eventually wake up.

"Today, Bri," Amanda said into her walkie talkie. "Sheesh, always the perfectionist!"

"That's a big 10-4, Ammie, on Perfectionist Man," came the reply with a squeal on the receiver. Amanda smiled. She sat at base camp checking the monitor. They had four video cameras running through the building. Two on the second floor in the area where Barnes had been attacked, one down the hallway from her and one in what used to be the morgue. Brian took his time getting them set just right. Secure. Focused on point. It made no sense to set up a camera that would slowly fall off its perch so what was recorded would slide out of view and he took his sweet time to make sure it was right.

"How's that?" he called. He was setting the last camera so that they had the whole second floor area at the end of the hallway covered from two different angles. If anything was going to happen there, he wanted every possible inch and angle covered.

"Looks great. I think we're ready."

"Good. Just another adjustment." Squeak. Squeal. God, sometimes she thought he did that on purpose.

"Come on, Bri. We'd like to get some dinner before the night's over."

"Food? The cameras are set, don't leave without me!"

They sat in a diner on Main Street waiting for Brian to decide what he wanted. He had been scanning the menu for at least fifteen minutes and when the waitress came back for the second time, Amanda took the menu out of his hands. "Forgive my brother. Food confuses him. He'll have a swiss cheese bacon burger, fries and a large chocolate milkshake."

The waitress looked over at Brian, smiling.

"Yeah, that's what I'll have." He took the menu out of Amanda's hands. After the waitress had gone to put in their orders, Brian leaned in toward the table and asked, "What the hell is up with that Joe guy?"

Dom eyed Brian over his coffee mug.

"I mean, he's definitely not being straight with us."

"Yeah," Dom said. He put his cup on the table and shook out a couple of sugar packets.

"I don't like him," Amanda said. "He's giving off this weird vibe."

"I think he's lying about the activity, too," Dom said.

"He's got a Ouija board on his kitchen table. You can't tell me that he hasn't used it. And there's a gun in his office desk drawer.

Not that other people don't own guns, but I thought we should take note of that."

"Fuck me," Dom said. "Now we have to seriously figure this out. Is tonight going to be safe? Do we have any reason to think he could be dangerous?" He looked at Amanda, hoping her sensitivities would jump in and point him in the right direction. As head of the team it was his final call, his responsibility to make sure they'd all be safe.

"I don't know," she said. "It's weird. I feel like I know him from somewhere but can't put my finger on it. I'm not sure if what I'm feeling is for him, from him, or just the sick nature of this place."

"I don't think he's dangerous," Brian said. "But I think we should keep an eye on him. And be aware, if he's used the spirit board that could ramp up activity. We already know the potential is there for something pretty negative. If he's opened up a portal, who knows what there could be? Anything could have crossed over. Or still could."

"True," Amanda said. "But it's too good of an opportunity to pass up. We'll need to go in extra protected. I think we need to get rid of that board, too."

"Now how are we going to do that?" Brian asked.

"I don't know," she shrugged. "But if he's been using it, it really needs to be disposed of."

"Holy water, Sis? You got some?"

She rolled her eyes. "No, Bri."

"Maybe that's something we need to keep with our equipment from now on."

"Shut up."

"I'm dead serious!" Brian said, then smiled. "Sorry. I am serious, though. If we're going to come up against these situations, we should be ready."

"There are other ways, Bri."

"One sec," he said, pulling out his phone. "Siri, how do you dispose of a Ouija board?"

Amanda grabbed his phone and turned it off. "Jeez, Bri. Get a grip. They can be buried, broken into pieces, saged."

"Yeah, but does it work?"

"I don't know. Haven't had to do it before."

Dom nodded. "Okay then. We go in as protected as we can be. If anything gets out of hand, we're out. Maybe we can convince Joe to give up the board."

Amanda and Brian stared at him. They all somehow knew that would never happen. Brian nodded, taking a long sip of his milkshake. He smiled. "Don't we need to all put our hands together and shout 'Go Team,' or something?"

Dom and Amanda broke out laughing and she kicked him under the table.

Brian settled in at base camp, making sure the monitor with the video feeds was at the best angle for his viewing. He had the voice recorders, EMF meter, digital camera and everything that Dom could want, laid out across the table. A couple of power bars and a bottle of water stood on the table next to him. He stretched and cracked his knuckles, ready to get down to business.

"Snacks? Already?" Amanda said.

Brian smiled. "If I'm going to be up all night, I want to be prepared. It's the boy scout in my blood."

She laughed. "More likely a tapeworm."

Dom looked at the monitors, checked the equipment. "Everything's got fresh batteries?" As if he had to ask.

"Yup."

He grabbed a voice recorder and a Mel-meter, handing them to at Amanda, and then picked up the camera. "Want to start in the basement? We can go through the building the same way Barnes did."

"Yeah. Sounds like a plan. I think it'll give us a better feeling for how the activity is going to go… or not…tonight."

"You're set, Bri?" Dom said.

"Yup!"

They tested their walkie talkies on the way down the stairs toward Joe's office.

The door was locked. "Now, that's odd," said Amanda. "He

knew we were coming back."

Dom knocked. "Joe?" he called. They heard some movement, the sound of breaking glass and cursing.

"Is everything okay in there?"

The door opened. Joe looked exasperated. Sweating. "Yeah. I dropped a glass."

"Sounded like it was thrown," said Amanda.

"Yeah? Well it wasn't," Joe said. He brushed his hand across his shirt and a faint line of blood wiped off. "I'm going to go lay down. My head is fucking killing me." He turned, walking back through to his apartment.

Amanda raised her eyebrows at Dom. He sighed. "Let's get at it. I don't want to be here any longer than we need to be."

Brian pulled on a pair of headphones and set the feed so he could hear Dom and Amanda's EVP session in the morgue. Office. Whatever you wanted to call it. It fascinated him that the asylum had its own morgue, but he guessed that was somehow typical of the time. If you had people, patients, living out their lives here…with doctors and examination rooms, you'd probably need a morgue at some point. But it still felt odd to him. A cool kind of odd.

He kept his eyes moving to the other video feeds. He knew it would be too easy to get drawn into watching Dom and Ammie, like a television show, and that wasn't what he was there for. Even though the cameras were recording, he was the go-between from any possible activity to his investigators. He had his finger on the pulse of the building and would communicate to them if something was up in another area. This was his forte and, damn, he enjoyed it. It was a shame they couldn't have camera'd Joe. He was creepier than the ghosts.

Brian ripped the wrapper off a power bar and looked around the lobby. He tried to see it as Barnes had. The photos were freaky but didn't do the place justice. It's hard to get full perspective from a photo. It twisted his brain to know he was in the same lobby as Barnes. Well, mostly the same. Torn down and rebuilt into an apartment building, but still. He had to be within ten to twenty feet of where the guy had set up his own base camp. It excited him but made him more wary to keep on his toes. He didn't want to tangle with whatever it was that had gotten to Barnes.

Forty-five minutes later, Brian's walkie came alive with a buzz. "Anything doing there, Bri?" It was Ammie. It was always Ammie. Dom tended to delegate things like walkie messages.

"Very quiet, Sis. Very calm."

"Here, too. Not quite right, but quiet. We're going to head down to the storage room, see if we can get anything there."

"Not the medical room? Further into Joe's apartment?"

"Definitely not. He's got a headache. Went in to lie down and I'm not disturbing him."

"Sounds good. Maybe later, if he's out and about."

"We'll see."

He knew the tone in Ammie's voice. It meant "no way in hell." That was fine. He'd acquiesce to her gut instinct any day of the week. Not that he'd tell her that. He smiled. Not that he ever would.

Amanda kept the voice recorder running as they walked through the dimly lit hallway. Once she started, she generally kept them running the entire night. Or until the recorder was full and then she'd start on the next one. They ran about six hours, so it didn't happen often. It was better than stopping after each EVP session and having to remember to pop them back on again for the next. And ghosts didn't necessarily communicate on cue. Sometimes their best EVP's came when they weren't trying for them. That voice as you walked up the stairs, or stray whisper while you were chatting with your team about dinner. It happened.

Dom snapped a series of pictures as they walked. When they arrived at the storage room, Amanda examined the outside mesh.

"Isn't it odd to have it set up like this? Doesn't look that safe."

"Not really. A lot of places do it. The mesh is actually pretty secure. Tough metal." He ran his fingers over it, tugging to show Amanda that it didn't budge. "Looks like whoever set it up had security in mind." He pulled the door open, Amanda right behind him. "Wanna hand me that wedge?"

Amanda looked around. "I don't see it."

"Can't be far."

She felt around, checking a couple of the shelves beside the door. Nothing.

"Wait…how about this? It's a little small but should work." She handed Dom a small piece of wood, almost like a tent stake. He tried it, giving the door a small shove.

"MacGyvered." The makeshift wedge held for a few seconds, then the door swung shut with a slam.

Amanda curled her lips. "MacGyvered," she said.

Dom shrugged. "Let's just get started."

"I hope there aren't any spiders," she said.

"You know there have to be a few," Dom said.

"As long as I don't see them, we're good."

They explored, shining their flashlights on the boxes already housed on metal shelves. Dom sat on the floor toward the far end of the room. Amanda slid in beside him, her back to the wall.

"Ready?"

"Yeah."

"Dom and Amanda, basement storage area. 9:15 p.m. Is there anyone with us tonight who would like to communicate? We come with no disrespect. We want to document your existence here, carry with us any messages you may have …"

Joe stood in the doorway to his kitchen. His hand was aching, but he couldn't remember what he had done to it. His temples throbbed as he struggled to keep ahold of his mind, his own thoughts. Black had descended into him more deeply than before. His pain expanded like a mushroom cloud. Nuclear. His last hope was that whatever Black had planned was quick and he pitied those ghost hunters.

"Dom?"

"Yeah?"

"You don't think that door locked when it slammed shut, do you?"

"Nah. Probably just has a tight spring. Who would have an automatically locking door on a storage room? People would carry in boxes and get stuck every time."

Amanda got up. "You know it's going to bug me until I check it."

"Bug you?" he chuckled. He could almost see her rolling her eyes in the dark. "I know. Go see."

She made her way around the shelving and tried the door. Nothing. It wouldn't budge. She tried again, figuring she didn't pull hard enough. Not even a rattle. "Um, Dom?"

"Yeah?"

"It's locked." She tried a few more times. The handle was securely in place and they were stuck.

"Are you kidding me?" He approached with his flashlight high, spreading light across Amanda and the door. "It's got to be stuck. Here, let me try." He gave her the flashlight and tugged the door handle. "Ridiculous. We're locked in."

"Maybe there's a key stuck around the inside here somewhere?" Amanda asked.

Dom felt around the frame of the door, getting a splinter in the process. "Damn it." He shook his hand. "Well, we can do our EVP session here by the door, and when we see Joe come out of the office, we can yell over to him."

"We could yell now."

"Claustrophobic?"

"I think he did this on purpose."

"What? Why would he?"

"I don't know, but doesn't it seem weird?"

"Coincidence. Something wrong with the locking mechanism, probably. Nothing a screwdriver couldn't fix." The angle of the flashlight accentuated the tension in in her jaw. "Come on, Amanda. What investigator doesn't envision getting locked in a creepy room during an investigation? It's a little cliché, I'll admit, but it's not the worst thing that could happen."

She gave a weak smile and turned off the flashlight. "Yeah, I guess you're right. At least there's not some axe wielding maniac in a clown costume waiting to strike."

Dom laughed. "Now THAT would be creepy."

"We could walkie Bri and let him know."

"Yeah, and then he'd go wake up Joe, who you know is already in a foul mood. I think we should wait, finish our time here, and then see about getting out. It's not like we don't have all night."

"You're right," she said, easing up. "Let's get back to why we're here." She dragged over a box and sat on it. Glancing at the recorder, she asked, "Are there any spirits currently laughing at our predicament?"

"I'm sure they all are."

Brian picked up his water bottle and took a swig. The power bar had hit the spot and he was ready to go for a few more hours. He watched the video feeds. A little slow but that was nothing new. Hopefully Dom and Ammie would be back on screen soon. They'd definitely hit his floor for a little while, but would want to spend the majority of the night upstairs. That would have to be the hot spot of the night, if they were going to get any activity.

"How's it going in the storage room, guys?" Squeak, squeal. Static. Typical walkie. He loved the sound of it. The feel. He was such a tech junkie. He waited about a minute, then tried again. "Base camp to storage room. Dom? Ammie?" This time the static was worse. It didn't sound as if he was putting out any signal.

"Odd," he said. He knew the walkies had been fully charged before they left; he had done it himself. But, it wasn't unheard of. Spirits could drain the batteries of any piece of equipment you could name, or there could be more mundane explanations. He started fiddling with the back of the walkie, then felt around in one of the equipment cases for a screwdriver. He didn't like being out of touch with his team, but he'd keep an eye on the feeds while he messed with the device. Once they saw they couldn't reach him they'd be up to check in anyway. It was one of the first rules of ghost hunting: Check in at base camp. Dead walkies were a small setback for the night but the place didn't have great, if any, cell reception either. Figures.

As he examined the wires making sure nothing had become disconnected, he tried to keep an eye on the monitor. He caught some movement on Camera One. Joe had come out of his apartment and was in the office. Brian set the walkie down. All of his attention was on Joe and what the guy was doing. Not that it should matter but he thought Joe was a whack job and couldn't turn away. Kind of like the car wreck you pass on the highway, bottlenecking traffic and trying not to be obvious as you stare.

Joe stood in his office. Brian watched in uncomfortable suspense, ready to pounce if something looked out of the ordinary. The man didn't seem as if he was going to do work; he was just standing there. So strange. Finally, after what seemed like forever, Joe turned toward the camera. Faced it, as if staring directly at Brian, and smiled. There was nothing right about the upward twist of his lips. It was like an awkward mask of a man. Joe shot finger guns at him and walked back into the apartment.

"Lunatic," he said under his breath. "The guy's a freaking lunatic." He shook his head and went back to what he was doing. Never before had they had to deal with someone like this on an investigation. Some clients would stay around while they set up the equipment, but most made themselves scarce during the actual investigation. Scared of ghosts or plain bored with the reality of it. Sure wasn't like the TV shows where there was a ghost around every corner, or a chair sliding across the floor…flashlights turning on and off in response to questions. He shook his head. Most investigations were hours sitting in a dark house, hoping for some sort of activity. 'Course that made it even better when you did find something, some proof of the paranormal. He put the walkie aside. It'd be easier to check when he had them all together.

Joe squinted. The light was too bright even with his sunglasses in place. It was time. He shifted from foot to foot and ran a hand through his hair, sick with anticipation. The tense knot in his stomach was tying and untying and he could feel the strength that Black was pouring into his veins. His anxiety lifted as what was left of him gave way to Black's control. The surge of Black's power was electrifying. His eyes went entirely dark and the lightbulb over the sink exploded. He smirked. Goddamn, he felt amazing.

Flexing, he pulled the butcher knife from the wall and slid it into the back of his pants, the handle resting against his waistband. His tee shirt covered it. Ready. It was time to get the vermin out of his fucking home.

He walked into the hallway, ignoring the camera in his office this time. He knew Brian would be watching. Curious. That was fine. It didn't matter. Brian didn't matter.

"Joe!"

He heard the echo of the name called from behind him. Not his name, but the persona he'd be using for a short while more. He continued the façade.

"Yes?" He turned toward the sound.

"Joe. We accidentally got ourselves locked in here. Would you get us out?" Dom said.

He grinned. "Sure, sure. It happens. I've got to get that fixed.

Give me a few minutes to get the keys." Turning, he went up the staircase and out of the basement.

He emerged into the lobby. Brian looked up from the monitor.

"Dom said the walkies aren't working, but he'll be up in a little while. They're almost done down there."

"Thanks. I was wondering what was up."

Joe gave him a thumbs up and continued down the hallway. Brian called out, "Hey, Joe?"

He turned.

"Do you have a minute?"

"For?"

"We were discussing your Ouija board at dinner."

"I don't own a Ouija board."

"Well, the one in your possession. Your friend's board," Brian said. Damn, this guy wasn't going to make it easy.

Joe smirked. "And?"

"Well," he paused. "You should consider getting rid of it. We thought it might be a good idea. If there's any activity…"

"There isn't."

"If there was, though, it could stem from the board. Your friend may have used…"

"Who the fuck do you people think you are to tell me to get rid of anything in my house?"

"I didn't mean any offense. Really. It was only a suggestion, in case we found anything tonight, or if you started having any activity. Something you might consider. Those things can bring loads of trouble. I felt…"

"You can go to hell," Joe turned on his heel and strode away.

"You've used it, haven't you?" Brian called after him. He knew he shouldn't have as the words left his lips and he cringed. He couldn't hold it back. Joe flipped him off and continued on. Brian watched the camera feed, curious as to what the man was doing. "What the…?" Joe moved in close to the camera and was messing with it. The feed went blank. "Yo, Joe! What the hell?" Brian called after him. He heard what he assumed was his equipment hitting the floor and the sound of the staircase door slamming closed. Fuck. What had he caused?

He stood, still staring at the monitor. Before he could run down the hallway to check things out, Joe emerged onto the second floor. What the hell was this guy doing? As Joe reached for Camera Two, Brian had had it. He ran for the closest stairs. He was going to stop this nut job before all the cameras were trashed.

Camera Two was on the floor at Joe's feet when Brian got to him. He shoved Joe out of the way and bent down to get his equipment. "What do you think you're doing?" He held the video camera out in front of him. "This doesn't belong to you!"

A shadow grew around Joe like a huge, black aura. The sunglasses were gone and the man stared at him with blank, dark eyes. Dead eyes. Cold and calculating as a shark with prey in sight. "It ALL belongs to me!" His voice was different now. Deeper, angrier. "YOU don't fucking belong here!"

Adrenalin pulsed through Brian, leaving a sick metallic taste in his mouth. This was going south like a freight train. "Okay, Joe. Okay." He backed off, taking slow steps backward. "You don't want us here, we'll go. Relax. We'll go. Don't worry about the cameras." The air was thick. Heavy. He almost puked when the stench of decay hit him. The shadow, the odor. God, he had to get out of here. The team had never run into an entity like this before. His eyes darted for exits, for protection.

Immediately Joe, or whatever it was, rushed him. He slammed against the wall, a cold hand around his throat; his feet kicking inches above the ground.

"Do you know who I am?" Joe paused for an answer while Brian clawed at the hand around his throat, trying in vain to get free. He leaned in close to Brian's face and let the words roll off his tongue, enunciating every syllable. "*You're fucked.*"

Brian's jaw dropped and recognition flooded him. The voice. That sick voice he had listened to over and over. The one from Barnes' recording. Terror gripped him more tightly than whatever was holding him and Joe filled with Black's satisfaction as if he had waited for that moment his entire life. For millennia. It was dizzying. It fed him.

Brian's eyes were locked on the eyes of the thing in front of him. The air was bone numbing cold and the eyes… they were locked onto his soul. He couldn't get any words out. His mouth worked, his throat on fire, but all sound was gone. The eyes bored into his brain and he could feel its darkness. In one deft movement, the Joe-thing pulled out the knife and plunged it into Brian's stomach. Brian's body reacted, arms flailing, trying to grab for the knife, legs trying to push off the wall and away.

The thing leaned in close to Brian's face. "You know," it whisper-growled. "If I leave the knife in you, there's a chance you'll make it." Brian closed his eyes, near unconsciousness and dreading what would come next. There was no air in his lungs to conjure a scream and he couldn't even vomit. He was in that threshold between crushing pain and a growing stinging numbness spreading out from the wound. His hands gripped the blade, sticky with his seeping blood. This momentary pause was an excruciating torture until the Joe-thing ripped the knife from his stomach and dropped him to the floor. Brian bent into a ball, gripping his stomach, trying to pull in gasping breaths like a fish out of water. Blood pooled under him.

Joe stood looking at the dying man at his feet with a sense of déjà vu. He wondered if anyone would notice that Brian had died in the exact spot where Barnes had first hit the wall. Barnes. The name still fueled anger within him. He'd release it on the two downstairs.

He dropped the knife on the floor. Wouldn't be needing that. The other two would be simple. Like fish in a barrel. He walked confidently down the hallway and headed to the stairs.

Amanda was the first to see Joe come out of the stairwell and turn toward them. Sauntering.

"Something's wrong."

"Amanda?"

"Something's really wrong. Get back…we need to get back."

Dom didn't question her and they moved into the shadows of the storage room, behind one of the shelving units. They ducked down. "What's up? What's going on?"

Amanda was shaking. "I don't know. It's wrong. Wrong. Dom, we have to get out of here."

"Amanda, we can't."

He had never seen her like this before. She was gripping his arm, her nails digging into his skin. Red half-moons of blood welled up.

"Oh, my God," she whispered. "I can feel them!"

Joe strolled closer to the storage room as perception shifted. Dull, dust filled sunbeams poured into the room where the patients waited. Some paced idly while others sat in chairs, staring. Humming. Rocking. A few faded souls, still in threadbare hospital garb, gave him a wide berth as their paths crossed. Some nervously averted their eyes and disappeared quickly into the ether, trying to avoid notice. They'd seen him before. Felt him. He appeared to them as James Borden, the original caretaker at New Castle, but they knew better. As abusive as Borden had been, this was worse. There was a black aura around him, an entity. A puppet master. And they had no desire to dance on his strings. A small girl in a pale dress shuddered as Joe's hand brushed her shoulder and she dissipated into the wall.

He took a step or two, arms outstretched. Teasing. Challenging. His lips curved upward in a self-satisfied sneer. He was trolling. Trolling for souls. The room emptied quickly. The last patient, a tall quiet man with sunken eyes tried to make a break past him, wanting to get to his room where he could hide in safety. It was the only place he had ever known, had called home. His sanctuary. Joe charged him, plunging his hand into the man's chest, enjoying his terror as the spirit exploded into black mist. Amanda's skin erupted in gooseflesh. Joe's perception shifted back to the situation at hand. The storage room. The intruders. It was time to clean house.

"I found my keys. They were on the second floor with Brian."

Amanda's blood ran cold. There was no way that Brian would have left base camp. "You know he wouldn't have gone upstairs alone. Not without telling us," she whispered.

Dom nodded. He squeezed the button on the walkie talkie. Nothing.

Closer now, Joe said, "I let Brian know you'd be upstairs in a little while. To check in with him. You know, since the walkies aren't working."

Amanda gave Dom a "how did he know?" look. He shrugged. This night was going incredibly wrong and he had to get control. The upper hand. He reached into the box beside him, hoping for a weapon of some kind. Anything that could protect them. Nothing. Gardening supplies. A hose. "Fuck," he said. He started going through the few boxes that were near him while Amanda grabbed the two closest to her. Nothing usable. Clothing, lightbulbs. Bars of soap. Exasperated, she shoved them away.

Joe stood at the doorway. "I'm sure you won't find anything in my boxes. But go ahead. Keep searching. I've got all night."

"We don't want trouble. Unlock the door and we'll leave," Dom said.

"Oh, I'll unlock the door, alright. But you won't be leaving. We need to have a little talk about why you think you have any right to be here."

"You let us in. You gave us permission," Dom said from the darkness.

"You had no right to even ASK to come here. You should have left well enough alone after you went through Barnes' house. Fucking trespassers. Interlopers!" He strode to his apartment door and grabbed something from inside. A tire iron. He swung at each of the dim hallway lights, glass crashing to the floor. "I don't need these to see," he said. "Do YOU?" The last one sparked as it shattered.

Joe flung open the door to the storage room, letting it slam shut behind him. He swung the tire iron, sinking it into deep dents on the boxes around them. Dom ducked and tried to cover Amanda. Joe closed in, slow and steady, with wide, wild eyes. His hands were wet with blood. Brian's. His. Nothing registered. Joe clung to life within Black but couldn't feel anything except pounding in his brain. There was a snake wrapped around his gray matter, pulsing. Throbbing. It was like every migraine he'd ever had stuffed into his skull at once and every swing brought him closer to finishing what Black had started. Toward paying back his debt. Every hit was a satisfying climax; a momentary reprieve from the excruciating pressure building in his head. He would take out the fuckers ahead of him. When they were dead, he would be released.

While Dom shoved one of the shelf units in Joe's way, Amanda dove for the door. She fought with the lock, battering at it with a hand trowel she had grabbed from a box. As it gave free, Dom pushed her through the opening, scrambling behind her. Joe matched pace with them, gaining as they stumbled through the hallway. He swung again, grazing Dom's back; the cold metal tearing his shirt.

The next blow landed squarely into Dom's spine. He dropped to the floor as Joe raised the weapon in a dramatic "in for the kill" motion. Amanda turned. She stared in shock until Dom yelled, "Ammie! Run!" He rolled as Joe struck, the tire iron connecting with his lower leg, shattering the bone. He let out a yell and tucked into a ball, holding his calf. With his other foot he kicked at Joe to distract him from Amanda.

Joe turned toward Dom, bending down to stare into the man's eyes. Dom, panting in pain, stared back. Joe smiled and whispered, "Water."

Dom felt the word slam into his brain as a weight bore down on his chest. His lungs were tight, heavy. Full. He was fighting for every shallow breath. Drowning. Everything started to swim before his eyes, darkness seeping in as he struggled to stay conscious.

He was six years old again, playing beside his parents' pool. Little Matchbox cars were lined up, driving in and out of the gravel along its edge. His cousin Carl was there. Carl was nine and big. Dom scooped his cars up.

"I want the black one."

"No." Dom scooped up his toys. Carl was a bully. "They're mine and I'm putting them away."

"I want it. Gimmie it. Now."

Dom turned, his cars clutched to his chest as a hand hit him square in the back. He fell forward into the water as his cars sank around him.

The chlorine invaded his senses; taste, smell, it burned his lungs. Everything was bright and blue, but which way was up? He fought the water, arms splashing, to find his way to the surface, senses on fire. Seconds ticked by and he didn't know up from down, left from right. Panic was exhausting him and he opened his mouth, taking a gulp of water instead of life-saving air. He was face down, almost floating, barely noticing the hands dragging him out of the pool, and in the background a woman screamed.

"Dom!"

Amanda's voice cut through the waters and he snapped back to the present, gasping, the pain in his leg prominent now that he could breathe again. Joe turned his attention to Amanda.

She ran. She knew he'd be on her in seconds. There was no escape. No running up the stairs and away, no getting to the car before she'd be dead in his hands. She saw the office door was open. Running in, she slammed it shut and locked it. But now she was stuck. Locked in a box. The only other door was in his apartment, closer to him and Dom. Leaving him out there made her weak in the knees and sick to her stomach. But she had to keep going. She couldn't let it derail her.

She worked the desk, pushing and pulling at it as quickly as she could, to move it in front of the door. "A-man-da," Joe called out. He was still down the hallway from her. "You can't get away, my dear. You realize that now, don't you? Locking yourself into my apartment?" He clucked his tongue. "A very bad choice. I might even say, *you're fucked*."

She closed her eyes. The coldness of that voice, that awful voice, ice picked her soul.

"Your brother's dead, A-man-da," he said. She hated how he drew out the syllables of her name. How he taunted her. "And you know, there are only two doors you have access to. Dominick is propped up on the one to my apartment. I've recently put a deadbolt on the outside of that door, or did you miss that? Some added security. I knew you'd want that when you came to investigate. Can't have you here all night and not be safe, now can I?"

He banged the tire iron against the wall, nearly at the office door. She couldn't stand there, couldn't wait for him to kill her. She was like a deer caught in the headlights and that had to change. She started digging through Joe's desk, yanking the drawers open and letting them slam to the floor. Brian had said there was a gun. Papers, papers. She pulled them out, throwing them around her. Where the hell could it be? She needed to find it. Even if it only slowed him down, that would be all that she needed.

The top right drawer was locked. Damn it. That's where it had to be. Now she needed the goddamned key. The only drawer left was the pencil drawer and she yanked it open, spilling the contents onto the floor. There, under the pens, was a little silver key. That had to be it. Almost unable to get it into the lock, she shoved and it turned. The drawer opened and she saw the gun. "Please, God, let it be loaded," she said.

The tire iron struck the office door. Amanda, nerves frayed, dashed into Joe's apartment.

"Come on, Ammie," she heard him yell. "That's what that dear, sweet shit of a brother called you, isn't it? You know how this is going to play out. Why not make it easy on yourself and open the door? We'll talk." Bang. Another hit.

"What are your sensitivities telling you about me now, A-man-da? Can you fucking FEEL ME?"

Amanda doubled over in the apartment as the blast of negativity hit her. A stench; a rotting aroma of death surrounded her. Worse than when she was ten and her parents pumped out their septic tank. A heavy, wretched odor that laid on your tongue if you opened your mouth. She retched. What *was* he? All she could sense was… black. Black. A name, an entity, a place. It was all the same, all wrong. The doorknob was shaking. Twisting, but still held by the lock. She closed the door to the apartment and went farther into the kitchen. Broken glass crunched under her shoes. What had he done in here?

"I know where you are, A-man-da," he said. "My kitchen isn't the safest place for you, you know. Don't you realize that's where I got the knife that I used on your brother?" He smirked.

Black

She recoiled from the name.

"He's here with me now. In me. IS me. One and the same. Good old Black. He wants you to know your death is not going to be quick or gentle, my dear. He's going to put you on a fucking spit."

She heard the lock snap as it broke. There was a loud slam as the desk was thrown against the wall. Things were being kicked around. She moved the gun from hand to hand. There was nowhere else to go. She positioned herself in the doorway to his bedroom and waited.

"Maybe we'll filet you on Joe's desk. It would do nicely as an autopsy table, wouldn't it? How I miss the morgue. No worries, though. It'll suit you just fine. We'll take our time with you. Maybe take you on his desk. It's been a while since Joe got off." He laughed. "Or should we kill you first? A little necrophilia never hurt anyone."

Black flexed, grasping Joe's chin and turning his head from side to side, cracking his neck.

She shivered. Everything went quiet and then there was a knock on the apartment door. Her legs were like water once again and she felt the pulsing negativity coming through the place. She tried to speak but couldn't. Her throat was tight; mouth dry. There was nothing to say anyway.

Knock knock knock. Her tension heightened. He wanted to torture her. Wanted to get her to the edge and shove her off the cliff. She stood stock still.

KNOCK KNOCK KNOCK. The hair on her arms was standing up and the air was filled with the electricity of a storm rolling in; dark clouds covering the sun and that air pressured silence before the heavens let loose. The door blew in and Amanda fell backward. He stood facing her, arms wide.

"Amanda, dear," he said. "What are you doing in my house?"

"I –"

"I told your brother he didn't belong here and look what it got him. You never should have come here."

He lunged and she stumbled backward, aiming the gun at him. Shaking.

"You know that won't hurt me, right? You'd be murdering an innocent man. Poor Joe," he shook his head. "His death will be on your conscience while I live on. Can you deal with that, A-man-da?" The voice was deep and calm and dead. He circled past the coffee table.

"No, it's on you," she said. "You caused all this."

"Pull the trigger, bitch. I'm tired of this asshole." Black pulled back for a half second so that Joe could see the gun and in that fraction of time he hoped she'd fire. He wanted that sweet fucking release from Black, but knew it had to be a trick. A tease. A dangling hope that would be yanked away in the last desperate moment. Black spoke, "It's kill or be killed, A-man-da. You. Him. Decide!" The entity dove at her. Amanda squeezed the trigger without taking her eyes off the thing coming at her. She pulled it again and again and again, afraid to stop until the gun was empty and Joe's body had collapsed on the floor.

Thoughts spun wildly through her mind. Brian, Dom, Joe. Her eyes darted around the room and she realized she was still holding the pistol. Dropping it onto Joe's couch, she stood in shock. What to do? 911? She tried her cell. No signal. But she knew that. Had known it. Where was Joe's phone? She skirted past his body to get to the office, terrified he'd reach out and grab her. She was numb. Terrified and numb, if that was a thing. Shaking and oddly calm. The entity had pulled back, pulled away, when she shot and she didn't sense it now. Couldn't feel it. Maybe she had a little time before it returned. But if that was the fact, she wouldn't be walking away from Black again.

She found Joe's landline. It was against the wall, hanging by its wire. Must've gone flying when he, it, pushed the desk out of the way. She fumbled with the receiver, dropping it twice, and dialed 911. She held her breath.

"911, what's your emergency?"

God, what do you say to that? An evil entity took possession of the guy running Forest View, maybe killed my brother and friend and I took him out with seven rounds from a gun I found, but he'll probably be back on a murderous rampage soon? Her mind was reeling.

"911, hello?"

"I - I need an ambulance."

"What's the address of the emergency?"

"Forest View, the new apartments."

"And what happened, what is the nature of the emergency?"

"A guy…the manager here…went nuts. He…attacked my brother and friend."

"Where is he now? Is he armed?"

"He…he's…here. Dead, I think. I shot him," Amanda said. The reality of the situation hit her like a bus and she dissolved into tears.

"Ma'am. The police and ambulances are on the way. Stay on the line with me until they get there. Okay? Are you with me?"

Amanda nodded. "Yes," she said. "I'm here."

She heard a moan, some movement, and crouched as quickly as she could behind Joe's desk. It was Dom. He had pulled himself along the corridor, making it to the office door.

"Dom? Dom!" she squeezed from behind the desk and ran to him. Bruised and bloodied, at least he was conscious. She could hear sirens approaching. "Help is coming."

"Ma'am? Are you there?"

"Yes. He's alive. He's here, oh, please hurry."

"He? Is that your brother?"

"No. No…oh, I don't know where Brian is! He must be upstairs."

"Stay on the phone. Don't go anywhere. The police will be there any minute and they will find him. Ma'am?"

"I – I hear the police now. Thank you for your help…"Amanda dropped the receiver into its cradle. She had to get to Brian. She had to make sure that he was…was okay. Not dead. She couldn't accept the thought.

Amanda ran, adrenalin fed, up the staircase to the first floor, circling and exiting onto the second. "Brian! Bri!" She saw a body on the floor at the end of the hallway and ran to within five feet of it. There, in a thick pool of blood, lay her brother. Her stomach flipped. Her big brother. She leaned against the wall, legs weak and arms around her belly. She stayed there a minute, maybe more. Time was a static blur. A television station that had gone off the air. A test pattern to stare at while that maddening high pitched hum bored into your brain. She stared at Brian, seeing and yet not seeing, her synapses firing on a thousand thoughts and none.

And then it hit her. The board. She needed to get that board. The thought superseded every other thought in her head. Her brother was dead because of *that board*. Dom was attacked… because of *that board*. Barnes was dead…because of *that board*. Black, his name twisted her stomach into a painful knot, came through *that board*. She had to dispose of it before anyone else was damned.

She made her way down into Joe's apartment. The terror still fresh, she gave him a wide berth. Amanda looked around the kitchen. Nothing. Brian had said it was on the table, she was sure, but it was empty. She pulled everything off Joe's shelves, racing against the approaching sirens. How would you tell the police you killed someone and then ransacked his shelves looking for a Ouija board? They'd lock her up for sure. But it wasn't there. It wasn't anywhere. Gone. Where could he have hidden it?

She felt a vibration, a movement, and something whizzed past her head. A steak knife imbedded itself in the opposite wall with a thud. The temperature around her suddenly dropped and the table shook. A tremble, at first, like a mild earthquake rumbling. Then stronger. Rattling everything on it to the floor. Amanda moved quickly, and escaped to Dom. It was time to flee. She'd been warned and she wasn't going to stay there and question it. She could sense, hear, a dark voice telling her to leave. There was no cliché "Get out" like in the movies. This was a "Get your fucking ass out of my space NOW." She took Dom by the shoulders and dragged him closer to the stairway. Tried. Adrenalin spent, she disregarded all the stories of moms lifting cars off their kids. This guy wasn't budging.

Police flooded the building, guns drawn. Once they were sure the area had been secured, the medics entered, assessing Amanda and Dom, while the police took her statement. An officer walked her upstairs, an arm around her shoulders. Her tears smeared across his uniform as he brought her outside into the fresh night air and the spotlights of the squad cars. Dom was loaded into the first ambulance and, as Brian's lifeless body was brought out on a stretcher, Amanda collapsed.

EPILOGUE

Amanda pulled VW Vinnie into the parking spot and shut off the engine. The bitter wind buffeted the car and the cold seeped in. She paused before picking up the package on the passenger seat, then gripped her scarf and shoved open Vinnie's door. Snow bordering on sleet pelted her face. She hated this weather. Pulling up the collar of her jacket, she power walked into the large building in front of her.

A double set of automatic doors whooshed open and closed behind her and she wiped her boots on the slushy welcome mat. She stomped her feet and went over to the desk. The receptionist pointed a disinterested finger at the visitor sign-in book. Amanda nodded. She was the first to sign in today and probably would be the only one. No one wanted to go out in this weather and few of the residents got many visitors on a good day. She gave a quick smile to the desk woman and took the elevator to the 3rd floor.

Dodging lunch carts and wheelchairs, she walked to room 302. It had become routine, over the months. The hardest was the first time she had visited, in the weeks after Brian's funeral. It had taken some time to find her, too. She knocked on the partially open door, waiting for a response that she knew wouldn't come, and walked in. The television was off, as were the lights. The usual. She gathered herself and put on her best smile. "Hi, Mabel!"

The old woman sat in a wheelchair beside her hospital bed, barely turning her head to look toward her visitor. She heard the words but they seemed so distant. She licked her lips. She recognized this woman, she thought. They had met before. Her mind was foggy, however, and it took an effort to pry through the mist. She sighed and sat back, vacantly looking in the woman's direction.

Amanda turned on a lamp and leaned in to give Mabel a hug. "I brought you something." She put the package on Mabel's bed tray and slid it over in front of her. "Thought you'd like it."

Mabel put her fingers on the brightly wrapped box, then dropped her hand into her lap.

"Let me get it for you." Amanda peeled the paper from the box and opened it, taking out a colorful hat. She knocked the box to the floor and put the hat on the tray.

Mabel's eyes took in the gorgeous shade of lavender with the deep purple sash. A peacock feather was tucked in at an angle. She felt the brim.

"There's a pin, as well," Amanda said, reaching into the box. She pinned the matching peacock feather to Mabel's sweater. The woman managed a smile at her. "The color suits you."

They sat for a few minutes, content. Mabel lifted a hand and pointed at the pitcher of water on the tray. Amanda poured her a small cup and handed it to her. She sipped. Slow, thoughtful sips, then delicately set the cup down. She rested her hand on Amanda's.

"Have… the nightmares… stopped?" It was a quiet whisper of a voice.

Amanda looked away, then to the floor. "No."

Mabel gave her hand a weak pat. They sat in silence for a while. It was like that sometimes. Others, Amanda would come in and tell her the things going on in her life. Her job, her friends. Dom. They had set aside ghost hunting, at least for now. It wasn't something either of them could face yet. Or who knew if they ever would. She couldn't deal with whatever might be lurking in a realm she couldn't see. A realm that had murdered her brother.

"Fear," Mabel said, "is crippling." She clenched and unclenched the edge of the hat. "Don't let him win."

"Didn't he?"

"Are you still here?"

Amanda opened her mouth to respond but thought better of it. Mabel ran her fingers along the peacock feather, letting the tendrils glide over the back of her hand.

"Would you like to try it on?" Amanda leaned in to take the hat and Mabel held up her hand.

"I…won't be going out," she said. "There's a storm coming."

"Oh, I think it's easing up."

"You need to go."

"What? Mabel, I just got here."

"It's time to go."

Amanda checked the window. "I don't think it's that bad."

Mabel looked her in the eye. "Go."

Amanda sighed, picking up her coat and scarf. She gave Mabel a hug before walking out of the room. "I'll come again. Soon," she said.

Mabel's eyes went to the window to see if she could watch Amanda leave, catch sight of the car turning out of the lot. When she looked back, the hat whisked itself off her tray and onto the floor, flattening as if someone had stepped on it. She shut her eyes and breathed as her mind clouded and the room turned cold. Her next visitor had arrived and his stay would not be pleasant.

GLOSSARY

Apparition - the ghost-like image of a person or animal.

EMF Meter - measures fluctuations in electromagnetic fields. Many people believe that spirits can manipulate these fields, causing unusual "spikes" or elevations in the measurements. The Mel-Meter is an EMF detector with a temperature sensor.

EVP - electronic voice phenomenon. These are sounds and voices found on electronic recordings that are attributed to spirits. Divided into classes, with Class A being the most clear and obvious.

Ghost box - a piece of equipment used for direct communication with spirits. It is generally a modified AM/FM radio that does a continuous scan through the band. It is believed that spirits can manipulate the energy and communicate through the device. Also known as a spirit box.

KII Meter - another type of EMF detector. The KII uses colored lights to indicate the intensity of the electromagnetic field.

Ouija Board - a flat board that has been painted with the alphabet, numbers 0 - 9, the words yes, no, hello and goodbye. Although marketed as a game for children, many consider it a communication tool for spirits. Also known as a spirit board or talking board.

Planchette - the small, usually heart shaped piece of wood or plastic used with a Ouija board. Participants place their fingers gently on its edges and wait for the planchette to slide across the Ouija board to spell out words, supposedly communication from spirits.

Portal - a crossing over point through which spirits can travel.

ABOUT THE AUTHOR

Barb Shadow is a paranormal investigator, researcher and mom, and lives on the East Coast with her kids, cats and dog. She cofounded the Sullivan Paranormal Society, an investigative team in upstate New York, and has appeared on numerous radio shows to discuss her experiences. Barb has kept a journal of her ghostly encounters for the last thirty years.

A Step Into Darkness, the first book in this series, was released in March 2018.

To find out more about Barb and to get updates on her upcoming titles, visit **barbshadow.com**. There you are able to follow her paranormal blog and contact her with any comments or questions you may have. She is always happy to connect with fans! Barb can also be found on Twitter @BarbsWriting and Instagram at barbshadowwrites.